"With its superbly nuanced characters, impeccably crafted historical setting, and graceful writing shot through with scintillating wit, Campbell's latest lusciously sensual, flawlessly written historical Regency ... will have romance readers sighing happily with satisfaction."—*Booklist, Starred Review, on What a Duke Dares*

"Campbell makes the Regency period pop in the appealing third Sons of Sin novel. Romantic fireworks, the constraints of custom, and witty banter are combined in this sweet and successful story."—*Publishers Weekly on What a Duke Dares*

"Campbell is exceptionally talented, especially with plots that challenge the reader, and emotions and characters that are complex and memorable."—*Sarah Wendell, Smart Bitches Trashy Books, on A Rake's Midnight Kiss*

"A lovely, lovely book that will touch your heart and remind you why you read romance."—*Liz Carlyle, New York Times bestselling author on What a Duke Dares*

"Campbell holds readers captive with her highly intense, emotional, sizzling and dark romances. She instinctually knows how to play on her readers' fantasies to create a romantic, deep-sigh tale."—*RT Book Reviews, Top Pick, on Captive of Sin*

"Don't miss this novel - it speaks to the wild drama of the heart, creating a love story that really does transcend class."—*Eloisa James, New York Times bestselling author, on Tempt the Devil*

"*Seven Nights in A Rogue's Bed* is a lush, sensuous treat. I was enthralled from the first page to the last and still wanted more."—*Laura Lee Guhrke, New York Times bestselling author*

"No one does lovely, dark romance or lovely, dark heroes like Anna Campbell. I love her books."—*Sarah MacLean, New York Times bestselling author*

"It isn't just the sensuality she weaves into her story that makes Campbell a fan favorite, it's also her strong, three-dimensional characters, sharp dialogue and deft plotting. Campbell intuitively knows how to balance the key elements of the genre and give readers an irresistible, memorable read."—*RT Book Reviews, Top Pick, on Midnight's Wild Passion*

"Anna Campbell is an amazing, daring new voice in romance."—*Lorraine Heath, New York Times bestselling author*

"Ms. Campbell's gorgeous writing a true thing of beauty..."—*Joyfully Reviewed*

"She's the mistress of dark, sexy and brooding and takes us into the dens of iniquity with humor and class."—*Bookseller-Publisher Australia*

"Anna Campbell is a master at drawing a reader in from the very first page and keeping them captivated the whole book through. Ms. Campbell's books are all on my keeper shelf and *Midnight's Wild Passion* will join them proudly. *Midnight's Wild Passion* is a smoothly sensual delight that was a joy to read and I cannot wait to revisit Antonia and Nicholas's romance again."—*Joyfully Reviewed*

"Ms. Campbell gives us...the steamy sex scenes, a heroine whose backbone is pure steel and a stupendous tale of lust and love and you too cannot help but fall in love with this tantalizing novel."—*Coffee Time Romance*

"Anna Campbell offers us again, a lush, intimate, seductive read. I am in awe of the way she keeps the focus tight on the hero and heroine, almost achingly so. Nothing else really exists in this world, but the two main characters. Intimate, sensual story with a hero that will take your breath away."—*Historical Romance Books & More*

ALSO BY ANNA CAMPBELL

Claiming the Courtesan

Untouched

Tempt the Devil

Captive of Sin

My Reckless Surrender

Midnight's Wild Passion

The Sons of Sin series:

Seven Nights in a Rogue's Bed

Days of Rakes and Roses

A Rake's Midnight Kiss

What a Duke Dares

A Scoundrel by Moonlight

Three Proposals and a Scandal

The Dashing Widows:

The Seduction of Lord Stone

Tempting Mr. Townsend

Winning Lord West

Pursuing Lord Pascal

Charming Sir Charles

WINNING LORD WEST

THE DASHING WIDOWS BOOK 3

ANNA CAMPBELL

Serenade Publishing

Cover design: By Hang Le

ISBN: 978-0-6483987-5-2

Print editions published by Serenade Publishing
www.serenadepublishing.com

Thanks to my friend Annie West for allowing me to borrow her name for my hero!

THE CHALLENGE

Richmond Park outside London, May 1820

Helena, Countess of Crewe, arrived at Lord West's picnic, determined to talk to her brother Silas. Since yesterday when she'd caught Silas on the point of seducing Caro Beaumont—in a greenhouse in full sight of anyone who cared to look, no less—he'd done an excellent job of evading her.

Well, his evasion ended right now.

With a purposeful step, Helena approached her brother as he rode in on his dapple-gray mare. She could already tell something was afoot. He looked brittle and alert, like a man on the eve of battle. She'd seen him like this when his botanical experiments verged on a major breakthrough.

While a groom led the gray away, Silas's hazel eyes

sharpened on Caroline's flashy curricle rolling across the grass toward the extravagant festivities. West had taken great trouble to create his riverside idyll, with cushions and divans in open tents, fine wines and exotic delicacies to tempt jaded appetites, and boats for pleasure trips. There was even a string quartet scratching away at the latest tunes.

"You can't run away from me forever, brother dear."

Silas cast Helena a sheepish look. "Save the scolding. You couldn't say anything that I haven't already said to myself." He sighed and ran his hand through his untidy tawny hair. "I don't know what got into me."

To her regret, Helena knew the answer to that. Overwhelming desire.

When she'd burst into the greenhouse, the lust in the air had woken long forgotten memories. From their first meeting, she'd been wildly infatuated with her late husband, Lord Crewe. Desire, however frustrated, had outlasted love by a long measure. Until her pride had sickened at sharing his attentions with any other woman who took his eye, and she barred him from her bed.

Catching Caroline and Silas in a torrid embrace had provided an unwelcome reminder that Helena hadn't always despised her profligate swine of a husband. "Caro means to have West. I'll tell you that much."

Her friend wanted a lover and had set her sights on Lord West, Silas's boon companion and Helena's first sweetheart. Helena had tried to warn Caro that the dissipated West was a dangerous choice. But the lovely brunette had the bit between her teeth, and there was no stopping her headlong gallop.

Until yesterday in the greenhouse, when it seemed Silas might make a late run.

"You two are being dashed unsociable," West said softly, prowling up on his long, powerful legs. His green eyes were watchful. "Save the family reunion for your own time. I've got a dozen footmen standing idle, ready to answer every whim. If you persist in loitering over here, you'll hurt their feelings."

Despite having long ago recognized West's many faults, Helena couldn't suppress a frisson of awareness. She reminded herself she didn't like overly handsome men—Crewe had looked like a Greek god until debauchery took its inevitable toll.

Vernon Grange, Baron West, was another handsome man, if in a very different style. He was the classic English aristocrat, tall and elegant, and with features so crisp and perfect, they could be carved from marble. Glossy black hair under a stylish beaver hat. A commanding aquiline nose. An air of effortless authority that always made her bridle like a half-broken filly.

"West," Silas said, and Helena searched in vain for any hostility in his greeting. With Caro's preference turning to West, lately Silas had been grumpy with his childhood chum. "You've been devilish fortunate with the sunshine."

That thin, expressive mouth curled in wry humor. "I have contacts in high places."

West bowed over Helena's hand and sent her a glinting smile from beneath his heavy eyelids. It was a rake's trick, designed to make a lady's heart beat faster.

"Down below more likely," Helena muttered, struggling to hide how her pulses jumped at his touch. Knowing it was a trick didn't seem to offer her immunity from its effects.

What the devil was wrong with her? She hadn't felt an ounce of attraction for Vernon Grange since she was a sixteen-year-old ninnyhammer. Perhaps she should blame her unsettled reaction on seeing Caro and Silas so intimately connected on that bench.

"Put away your barbs, my prickly lady. It's too nice a day for sniping."

Coolly she withdrew her hand. "I'd imagined more guests, my lord."

The gathering comprised West, Helena, Silas, Caroline, a couple of West's rakish friends, and Fenella Deerham.

"The numbers are sufficient to my entertainment." Under the winged dark brows that added a satanic touch to his good looks, West's regard was searching. "Yours, too, I hope. You didn't ride?"

"No." Given the failure of her plan to quiz Silas on the drive to Richmond, she was sorry she hadn't come on horseback. It was so long since she'd had a good run, and this wide field beside the Thames offered scope beyond anything in Hyde Park.

"I have a spare horse."

Silas shuffled sideways to keep a better eye on his beloved. Caro glanced their way, stiffened, and headed swiftly in the opposite direction.

"Helena?" West said when she didn't respond. "I brought you a horse to ride."

She stopped watching her brother and met West's amused eyes. He was a man society fawned over—handsome, rich, from an old family. People were more inclined to hang on his every word than drift off in his presence. But he'd always worn his consequence lightly. A lesser person might find her erratic attention an insult to his vanity. Vernon Grange merely thought it funny. She'd always liked his lack of conceit, thorny as relations had become since she'd abandoned her girlish *tendre.*

"I can't ride astride. Even in Richmond that would cause talk." She fought to rise above the antagonism he always stirred. Crewe and West had been bosom bows at Oxford. She'd never forgiven West for introducing her to the man she'd so disastrously married. "But thank you for offering."

"You used to ride astride when you were a cheeky schoolgirl in plaits and a muddy pinafore."

"I used to do many things." A chill entered her voice. "But wisdom has a grim habit of following after reckless decisions."

His amusement faded. "Not always."

"No, not always." The ghost of her late husband hovered. Charming, deceitful, self-centered. And destructive—to himself most of all.

"I've missed seeing you on a horse, Hel," Silas said absently, still watching Caro, who had joined Fenella on the far side of the field.

West made an effort to lighten the tone. "I arranged this picnic purely for the pleasure of seeing you flying across the grass on the back of a galloping horse."

Oh, dear, that wasn't what she wanted to hear. She'd imagined he'd put this party together to further his pursuit of Caro. Helena didn't want West *noticing* her. For years, he'd been content to treat her as a distant acquaintance. "Really?"

"Yes, really. It's been a fancy of mine since I saw you restricted to a trot in Hyde Park. The experience was most uncongenial for an observer. You looked like someone was strangling you. Slowly."

She frowned, resenting that West made her the focus of his attention. And that his conclusions were so accurate. "Town isn't the place to ride neck or nothing. I'll soon be back at Cranham."

West signaled to a groom. "Such a pity."

"That I'm leaving London?"

"No, that you don't want a good gallop, when I went to such trouble to bring you a suitable mount—and a suitable saddle."

The groom led a pretty chestnut mare toward

them. Helena immediately noted the gleaming sidesaddle. Her hand curled at her side as if it already held a crop. Despite her misgivings about the man offering the favor, she itched to throw herself onto the lovely horse. The groom passed the reins to West, bowed and left.

West's smile was mocking. "If you deny me, I'll think that you don't like me."

She ran a gentle hand down the Arab's jaw and bit back a sigh of longing. The mare truly was a darling. "I don't."

That wasn't completely true. Her feelings for West had always been more complex than mere antipathy. When they were children, he'd been her hero. Shreds of that fondness lingered, although she'd long ago recognized that he was cut from the same cloth as her depraved husband.

"Ouch."

She studied West, as with unconvincing nonchalance, Silas wandered off in Caro's direction. "You don't believe me?"

West shrugged. "Explaining exactly what I believe requires more time and privacy than we now enjoy. Even if you insist on seeing me as the enemy, I hope you'll still accept Artemis as a gift."

"Gift?" Helena stared at him, appalled. "What on earth do you mean? I can't take such an extravagant present. Have some sense, West."

He stood unmoved by her refusal, tall and lean in

his immaculate dark blue coat and fawn breeches. "Nonetheless, she's yours."

"That's…" Helena struggled to understand what lay behind this ridiculous and inappropriate gesture. West had been out in society all his adult life. He knew how the world would interpret his generosity.

His gaze remained unwavering on her face. "Yes."

"Yes, what?" she snapped, although she had a sinking feeling she knew.

"Yes, it's a declaration of intentions."

Horror flooded her. She faltered back across the grass as if he'd made an unwelcome physical advance. "This isn't funny."

"I'm deadly serious."

"Then you're wasting your time." She straightened and glared at him. Her mind worked a thousand miles an hour to make sense of this abrupt alteration in their dealings. "I was a rake's wife. Be damned if I'll be a rake's mistress."

The tension vibrating between them upset the mare, and she shifted nervously. West patted Artemis's glossy neck in reassurance.

"I know you're frightened, Hel." His voice was low and deep, and Helena resented that he sought to reassure her, too.

Her temper sparked, not least because he used her childhood nickname. "Devil take you, nothing frightens me."

Despite her brave words, fear curdled her stomach

and tasted sour in her mouth. She didn't want Vernon Grange to pursue her. She wanted to stay safe in her lonely little eyrie. Nine tempestuous, miserable years with Crewe had left scars that had hardly healed in the eighteen months since his death.

"Love frightens you."

"You don't know what that word means."

"Let's not quarrel." Calmly he offered Artemis's reins. "Not today when I've worked so hard for your enjoyment. Come riding with me."

She glowered at his hand as if it held poison. "That's it? 'I want you as my mistress, but we won't fight about it, and now come for a canter?'"

His laugh made her itch to slap him. "Pretty much."

"That's not good enough."

"My dear Helena, if you require a more emphatic declaration, I'm prepared to make my plans public. I'm only holding back to protect your reputation and help you become accustomed to my interest. If I kiss you in front of all these people, your fate is sealed."

"As if I'd let you kiss me."

"As if you could stop me."

Curse him, now he'd mentioned kisses, she couldn't stop staring at his firm, sharply defined lips, and wondering what he'd learned since those clumsy, but pleasurable experiments in the summerhouse.

She reminded herself that anything he'd learned, he'd learned through unbridled lechery. To her shame, that didn't dilute her fascination.

"What about Caroline?" Her voice was flat. "Or are you covering your bets and chasing both of us?"

Humor lit his eyes, and he glanced across to where Caro fought a losing battle to avoid Silas. "On my honor, you're the only woman I'm interested in. Caroline has her own fish to fry."

Resentment and apprehension curdled in Helena's belly. "I'm not listening to this nonsense."

With a contemptuous flick of her blue skirts, she whirled away. She wished she'd never come to this cursed picnic. Since reaching adulthood, she hadn't spent much time alone with West. That was clearly a good thing.

"Don't go." He caught her arm, holding her without force. Of course, after all that worldly experience, he knew how to handle a woman. "You'll kick yourself if you don't try Artemis."

She glared at him, loathing his effortless confidence and unabashed sexual allure. Loathing that he was right—about the horse at least. "I'd rather kick you."

A huff of laughter escaped him. "I'm sure you would. If I let you go, will you ride? Artemis is very sensitive. She thinks you don't like her either."

"Fool." Despite everything, a trickle of warmth softened the insult.

"That's not in question," he said, and she unwillingly remembered how once she'd enjoyed sparring with him.

"I'm not dressed for riding."

He glanced at her royal blue day dress with its jaunty gold military braid. "You'll do. And you're wearing half-boots."

Good Lord, a man had a woman in his sights when he noticed what she was wearing. This conversation became more alarming by the second. "West—"

"I'm not suggesting we ride to Cornwall. You're adequately fixed for a short run. I'd say different if you were done up in that devilish becoming red frock you wore to the Oldhams' ball on Tuesday."

Good Lord doubled. West really was paying attention. Perhaps he meant this tomfoolery about making her his mistress. "I'm not—"

"Please."

She sighed, the fight leaving her. He'd always been a stubborn sod. She wouldn't get rid of him—or manage to finish a sentence—until she rode the mare. "If you promise to stop acting like a lunatic."

This time his laugh was free and untroubled. "I promise to behave for the next half hour."

Heads turned in their direction. Helena stiffened with renewed wariness. She didn't want their names connected. After all, gossip was the fuel that powered the season.

She let him toss her into the saddle. Helena couldn't control a shiver when his hands closed around her waist. Blast him. And blast Silas and Caro, and their flagrant session yesterday.

Artemis shifted, sensing her rider's disquiet, but

settled when Helena took the reins. A groom brought up the stamping brute of a bay, familiar from the ride in Hyde Park. That early morning when West had been indiscreet enough to mention Helena's adolescent passion to Silas and Caro.

Until that day, Helena hadn't realized he remembered that turbulent summer. Given that West had been notorious for his wenching ever since, she'd imagined he'd long ago forgotten those innocent embraces.

Because for all their heat and fervor, they had been innocent. A year later, she'd gone to Crewe's bed a virgin. Not that the cur she'd married had deserved the honor.

Before West mounted, she urged Artemis to a gallop. The mare responded gallantly, and the restrictions and exasperations of London life vanished in a second.

Damn West, he was right. This was what she was born for: speed, the wind in her face, freedom. Freedom most of all.

She gave a joyful laugh as Artemis settled into a steady run that promised to take them to China and beyond. Helena was so elated to be on the back of a spirited horse that she didn't even mind when West thundered up behind her.

Over the lush green grass they rushed, and Helena tasted genuine happiness. She only drew rein when Artemis at last began to tire.

Turning to West, she couldn't contain her exhilaration. "That was marvelous. Thank you."

He stared at her as if he'd never seen her before. For once, no devil of laughter lurked in his green eyes. "This is how I always think of you. Strong and exuberant. The way you were as an impetuous girl. This is how you should stay, rather than wrapped up in stifling convention, pretending you're like everyone else."

Abruptly her euphoria drained away. She hadn't heard him sound so sincere since those ecstatic weeks at Woodley Park, when she'd imagined herself in love with him. He didn't sound like the shallow man she'd judged him to be. He sounded like someone who took the trouble to know her.

The fermenting fear in her stomach built to terror.

Long ago she'd placed Vernon Grange in a box marked "hazardous." And that was where she wanted him to stay. "I had no idea you thought of me at all, let alone *always*," she said repressively.

Something that might have been regret shadowed his features, before he resumed his lazy manner. He hadn't been a languid boy. He'd been vivid with passion and enthusiasm. But then so had she. Her verve hadn't survived her marriage.

"What do you think of Artemis?"

Helena wanted to dismiss West's choice of horse, if only to avoid admitting that in arranging that glorious gallop, he knew her better than she knew herself. But she couldn't lie about such a superb creature.

"She's a dream." Then went on when satisfaction sparked in his eyes. "Can I buy her from you?"

"She's not for sale," he said curtly. The bay snorted and shifted, as if West tightened his grip on the reins.

"That's a pity." Helena leaned down to pat Artemis's satiny neck. "I love her already."

"She's not for sale because she's already yours."

"West," Helena began in a warning tone.

He raised a hand in a conciliatory gesture. "But I'll keep her for the moment."

"You'll keep her because I haven't accepted her," Helena retorted, stifling a pang. If only the price of taking Artemis wasn't so high.

"No, I'll keep her because you haven't accepted *me*," he said. Then added with an edge, "Yet."

Before Helena could muster the words to put him in his place, he wheeled his great monster of a horse around and galloped back toward his guests.

LETTERS

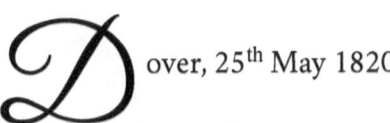over, 25th May 1820

My dearest Helena,

Man proposes, and God disposes. Or at least Lord Liverpool does. According to our esteemed prime minister, my private pursuits must play second fiddle to the nation's needs.

I'm off to St. Petersburg to solve a horrid diplomatic tangle for the Tsar. A horrid tangle that threatens to play havoc with the India trade, so you can imagine how the East India Company is up in arms about it all.

I have no idea how long I'll be away. Liverpool said it could be as much as three months.

Damn it, Helena, the ship is about to sail to catch the tide. I have so much to say to you, most of which I know you're not ready to hear. I'm sadly aware that we have years of past hurts to bridge.

Write to me at the embassy in St. Petersburg.

Yours in haste.
West

P.S. I'm consigning Artemis to your care. If you won't accept her as a gift, consider her a loan. No, as an expression of intentions that at present I'm too far away to make reality.

London 26th May 1820

Lord West,
I wish you safe and swift travels – straight to the devil!

You have no right to call me your dearest, and only a regrettable childhood association gives you the smallest right to use my Christian name. Don't bother writing to me. I won't read your letters. And I won't set up a cozy correspondence as though we're anything more than the merest acquaintances. The thought of the nation's welfare in your careless hands gives me the shivers. It's even less likely that I'd entrust my person to you.

Sir, as far as I'm concerned, the Russians are welcome to you.

With no respect whatsoever.
Helena Crewe

P.S. Most unwillingly, I've found Artemis a place in my stables. Inquiries indicate you have closed up your London house for the duration of your absence. I'm now making arrangements to send her down to Cranham. Your lack of care for her is yet another indication that you're the same irresponsible boy you always were.

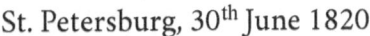

St. Petersburg, 30th June 1820

My lovely Firebrand,

Your sweet missive was waiting when I reached St. Petersburg yesterday. Thank you from the bottom of my heart. Your words had the bracing effect on my spirits that I'm sure you intended. In comparison, I found myself thinking fondly back on the hellish journey across the Continent.

I hope the letters I wrote on the way have warmed you up a little since then. It's a good thing I like a challenge—which must be why they sent me on this pestilential quest to solve Russia's quarrels in the first place.

We arrived last night, and so far I've had little

chance to see the city. We're billeted in a pink and white palace on the Neva, with icing sugar decoration and big china stoves in every room. It doesn't get dark at night at all. There are canals everywhere. It's a most elegant place. I wish you were here to share your acerbic opinions and remind me I haven't wandered into a fairy tale. Although I imagine once the Tsar's negotiations start, any magic will vanish in a puff of bureaucratic pomposity.

I also wish you were here because I find myself missing you and all your prickles. I'll think of you as my dear little hedgehog. There, does that not melt your heart?

Tomorrow the ambassador presents me to his Imperial Majesty, the Tsar. I'm sure you'll want to hear about that, so I hope you won't tear up the letter the moment arrives.

With my dearest wishes.
West

P.S. I hope you're making sure Artemis gets plenty of exercise, and you're riding her, not some brick-handed groom who won't appreciate the highly strung miracle she is.

London, 28th July 1820

My lord,
Kindly desist from writing to me. As I consign any correspondence from you to the drawing room fire, all you're doing is supplying me with exotic kindling. Your activities are of no interest and I'd prefer that we returned to being polite strangers. That relationship has served us well since we both grew up. At least I grew up. Nothing I've seen indicates that you have.

Not yours.
Helena, Lady Crewe

P.S. As if I'd employ a heavy-handed groom. The unhealthy Russian air must have rotted your brain.

Outside Moscow, 3rd September 1820

My beautiful sweetheart,
How villainously those of high degree lie to their humble servants. I'd hoped to be home by now and telling you in person of my unending admiration. Even as an impossible brat who was either hanging around the stables getting underfoot, or hidden in the corner

of the library with your nose in some dusty volume, you were something special.

I know I have much to atone for—what I can't bear is that you feel I'm responsible for Crewe's disgraceful behavior. We were both disappointed in him, although as his wife, you bore the brunt of his extravagance, drunkenness, and lechery. In comparison, a friend's disillusionment pales to nothing.

To Hades with me. I swore I'd wait until I saw you to address the matters that rise like a wall between us. It's a wall I'm determined to scale. I imagine you waiting on the other side, like a captive princess.

As you can see, all this Russian romance is softening my head. Of course, my Helena is no captive princess, but a warrior maiden. A man needs all his wit and weaponry to lay siege to her.

The negotiations crawl along without noticeable progress. Every day, the Tsar goes hunting through birch forests, beautiful with coming autumn.

Next week, we travel south to the Crimea without His Imperial Majesty. He feels his government—and the English interloper—needs to know the lay of the land down there to understand the full implications of this tangle. He's off to the Congress of Troppau to strut on the world stage and enjoy some Western luxury. We might make headway without his royal interference.

This is a strange, beautiful, stirring, half-barbaric country, for all its wealth. I'd love to bring you here one day. I think your untamed spirit would feel at home. As I ride out every dawn, I imagine you galloping at my side, the way we galloped at Richmond half a world away.

I hear Silas and Caro are more wrapped up in each other than ever. He really should marry the girl. And Fenella has a thousand admirers, but doesn't give a fig for any of them. I also hear you and Lord Pascal have been seen together several times at the opera. I know he's handsome, my darling, but the fellow will bore you to death once you've stopped looking at him and started listening to him. You need a man to keep you on your toes. A man undaunted by your magnificent brain.

There's a much more suitable lover available, although he's currently occupied abroad on international affairs.

I hope when you sleep, you dream of me.

Your fervent admirer
West

P.S. When it comes time to put Artemis to stud, allow me to suggest my stallion Perseus. They will have beautiful, spirited offspring.

Cranham, Wiltshire, 10th October 1820

Sir,

Despite repeated requests to refrain, still you pester me with unwanted confidences and reflections. Again I tell you they—like you—are of no interest. It seems cursed unfair that you are much more annoying at a distance than you ever were in London. The Russian doxies mustn't keep you as amused as our local variety always has. I hesitate to recommend sin, but, my lord, you need to fill those long Russian nights with something other than the cold ashes of an old dalliance. If sin has palled through overfamiliarity, permit me to suggest that you take up knitting.

Again, I insist that you cease this stupid game and leave me in peace.

Hopefully for the last time.
Lady Crewe

P.S. Artemis remains your horse, even if she's been eating her head off in my stables for the last six months. I begin to think you sent her to me as an economy measure. The arrangements for breeding her are none of my concern.

London, 1st December 1820

West, old chum!

Congratulate the happiest man in England. Nay, the world. My glorious Caro has agreed to become my wife, and I'm ten miles high in the sky as a result.

Can you tear yourself away from the bears and the balalaikas and the Cossacks long enough to come home and stand up with me? Our plan is to have a quiet wedding at Woodley Park on Valentine's Day. Forgive the sentimental choice of date, but I've become disgustingly sap-headed since my beloved consented to marry me. Then a short honeymoon before Caro and I leave with the Horticultural Society's expedition to China.

The dates are fairly set in stone, so I'll understand if noblesse obliges you to stay shivering in the snow and ice, running the Tsar's errands.

But given you've been my best friend since I could walk, I'll be dashed sorry if you can't make it to Leicestershire to raise a glass in my honor and make an embarrassing speech at the wedding breakfast.

Anyway, let me know when you can. There's nobody I'd rather have at my side when I pledge my life to the woman I love.

Yours, etc.
Stone

CHAPTER ONE

The Wooing

Woodley Park, Leicestershire, February 1821

*H*elena strolled out of her childhood home into a perfect winter morning. The air was cold enough to make her lungs ache, but the sky was pure blue and the light so clear that everything looked new minted. She stopped in the empty stable yard and sucked in a deep breath. The worries and stresses of city life drained away.

She was a countrywoman at heart. Always had been.

Instead of living in London most of the year, she should spend more time on her estate, Cranham. Especially with Caro and Silas traveling, and Fenella planning her wedding to Anthony Townsend.

How she'd miss having her friends close by. She didn't exaggerate when she credited the other members of the dashingly named Dashing Widows with saving her life in those dark days after Crewe's death in a hunting accident. Not that she'd missed the philandering bastard, but nine turbulent years as his wife had left her bitter and withdrawn. Caro and Fen had reminded her she was more than just a foolish girl who had wed a rake and lived to regret it.

Now Caro and Fenella looked forward to their own happiness, which was wonderful. *Except...*

Except Helena felt left behind, still mired in the past. Sighing, she tapped her crop against her thigh. Enough self-pity. She'd had a bellyful of that, married to Crewe. With her friends embarking on new lives, she needed a fresh purpose, something to carry her through the inevitable loneliness.

And she had plenty to be grateful for. She was her own woman with resources to take any path she chose.

Luckily by the time her father drew up the wedding settlements, he didn't trust the man his daughter had chosen. The late Lord Stone had made provision for Helena to have exclusive use of a substantial portion of her dowry. Within the first few years of marriage, Crewe had gone through his own fortune, as well as every penny he'd gained in wedding her. Without her father's foresight, she'd have been destitute. Then last year, an inheritance from a blue-stocking aunt had turned her from comfortable to wealthy.

There was time enough to decide which worlds to conquer. Today she had a lovely morning, a fine horse waiting, and familiar haunts to revisit.

With a light step, she headed for the stables. "Good morning, Becket," she said as the head groom appeared, pushing a laden wheelbarrow.

"Miss Helena," he said, forgetting that she was no longer the family's coddled daughter, but the much grander Countess of Crewe. If only she could forget, too. "We've missed you about the old place."

His lined face creased in a greeting that reminded Helena how happy she'd been growing up at Woodley Park. The estate had been Eden until the arrival of a snake, in the form of Gerald Wade, Lord Crewe.

Becket had put her on her first pony before she could walk. He must be over eighty, but Silas couldn't convince him to accept a comfortable retirement. Becket vowed that while the Nash horses needed care, he'd stay on duty.

"Did Artemis settle overnight?"

"Aye. Like a champion. A right fine little mare she is." His eyes sharpened. "Comes from Shelton Abbey, don't she? Has the look of old Shah Persis."

Helena's sallow skin didn't hold a blush, but unaccustomed heat burned in her cheeks. "I bought her from Lord West earlier this year."

"The Granges don't like to share their best horses. You was a lucky 'un, then."

"Yes, I was." She hoped that West, when he returned, would reconsider selling the mare and change her lie into the truth. Lord West might annoy and trouble her, but Artemis was a joy.

Becket bobbed his head and trundled away out of earshot. When Helena entered the stables, Artemis stretched her neck over the loosebox door and whickered in welcome.

"Hello, lovely girl." Helena extended half a wizened apple on her palm and smiled as Artemis's velvety nose brushed her skin in equine greed. When she scratched behind the Arab's ears, they pricked forward in encouragement. "Did you miss me?"

"Like the very devil."

The baritone drawl made Helena jump and drop the other half of the apple. Artemis wasn't pleased.

Nor was Helena.

She closed her eyes, inhaled a breath of hay-scented air, prayed for composure, and turned. A tall, dark man leaned one broad shoulder against a post in the central aisle. He watched her with unwavering concentration.

"Lord West," she said coolly. "Still sneaking up on people, I see. You could give a cat lessons."

Sardonic humor curled his mouth and made him dazzlingly attractive, damn him. Her silly heart had started to race the moment he spoke. Sheer surprise, she told herself staunchly.

"I'd rather give you lessons."

She didn't pretend to misunderstand. "Better take the time to learn a little humility. I told you I wasn't interested."

"Even after I wrote you all those fascinating letters?"

"You're most welcome to go back to writing. I'll go back to ignoring you."

"A little difficult when we're under the same roof until the wedding."

Oh, no. Although she knew Silas had asked West to be his groomsman, the coward inside her had hoped that her bugbear would stay in Russia. "You make it sound so scandalous, when you know it's perfectly respectable."

"A man can live in hope." He straightened and sauntered closer with that long, smooth stride that she remembered so well. Except now she had a chance to see him in stronger light, a gasp of dismay escaped her. "West, you're not well."

His winged brows drew together in annoyance. "Like hell I'm not."

"You look dreadful." It wasn't altogether true. He'd lost a lot of weight in the months since they'd last met, and he was worryingly pale. But extreme thinness emphasized the purity of his bone structure, and in his striking face, the dark green eyes glittered with familiar wickedness.

"Why, thank you."

She reached to take his arm before she remembered that they were no longer friends, hadn't been friends in close to a dozen years. "You shouldn't be prowling around, trying to prove your rakish credentials. You should be in bed."

He was still smiling, but now she saw the effort it took. "I thought you'd never ask."

"Stop it, you fool," she snapped, shoving hesitation aside and grabbing his arm. She tugged him toward a narrow bench against the wall.

"Ah, such a fond greeting, my love." Despite his sarcasm, he couldn't hide his relief as he sat and rested his head against the wall behind him.

He was a ghastly color, and he was breathing unsteadily. Helena couldn't vanquish a feeling of unreality. West was a force of nature. He always had been. Surely no mere physical weakness could sap that titanic energy. "I'll fetch a doctor."

As he closed his eyes, his long mouth turned down. "Don't you dare. I've seen more than enough damned quacks in the last few months."

"When did you get back from Russia?"

"Two days ago."

"You traveled like this? You're raving mad."

This time sweetness tinged his smile. "Had to."

"I know you're Silas's best friend." From her earliest breath, West had been woven into her life. He'd been her first dance partner. He was the first boy she'd kissed. And when he'd introduced a handsome young man to her family as a capital fellow, nobody had bothered to check further into Lord Crewe's background. "But he won't thank you for killing yourself to be at his wedding."

"Not here for Silas." West's answer emerged in fits and starts. "Here for...you."

With every word he spoke, she became more concerned. He sounded like these short, staccato sentences were all he could manage. With a pang, she recalled how he'd provoked her at the picnic last spring. This was a different man.

Except apparently he was just as stubborn. And just as set on seducing her.

"I'll still be here in a couple of weeks," she snapped, then cursed herself for offering any shred of encouragement.

Another faint smile. His color was a little better, but he looked horridly ill. Fear coagulated in a cold lump in her stomach. Not of his powers of persuasion this time, but that she might lose him. For nearly half her life, she'd been angry with West, but that didn't mean she was ready to accept a world without him.

"Will you?" he asked.

"Of course I will. Where the devil else would I go? Mars?"

"Paris. New York. Timbuctoo." He snatched a shallow breath. "Lord Pascal's bed."

She should have expected this. West's fuming displeasure had been apparent in those unwelcome, irritating, marvelous letters that she'd insisted she wouldn't read.

During this last year, London's handsomest man had occasionally escorted her in public. The admission that Pascal meant nothing to her hovered on her lips, but wisdom kept her silent. "It's none of your business whose bed I sleep in."

What little color West had regained leached from his skin. He looked like an effigy on a medieval tomb. When he raised his hand, she automatically took it.

"Good God, West, you're burning up."

"You have no idea." He pulled her down beside him. "Tell me I'm not too late."

"Too late for what?" Whatever was wrong with him, it was serious.

"Don't play coy, Helena. It's never been your style." His words came more easily. "Are you and Pascal in love?"

She gave a dismissive snort. "I don't believe in love."

At last West opened his eyes. That green gaze blazed with fever, and determination. His illness hadn't totally banished the domineering earl. "You did once."

"When I imagined myself in love with Crewe?" she asked in an acid tone.

Her parents had been unable to prevent her headlong rush to disaster. They'd told her she was too young, and that Crewe was a wastrel and a rake, but his sins added to his dark glamour.

She'd recognized her mistake on their wedding trip

to Devon when she'd caught him rogering the inn's chambermaid. From there, things had only gone downhill.

"Once you imagined yourself in love with me."

"It's clear I was utterly brainless when I was young."

"Cruel goddess," he said without force, then his voice turned thoughtful. "Not brainless, but ardent, and eager to launch into life."

"Brainless."

"Incautious. Headstrong. Passionate." His grip on her hand tightened, and like an idiot, she didn't pull free. If he'd been his usual king of the universe self, she'd find no difficulty sending him away with a flea in his ear. But his illness made him cursed vulnerable, and she hated to kick a man when he was down.

"Brainless."

"Adorable."

She gave a snort of sour amusement. "I can't have been too adorable. You forgot me easily enough."

"I never forgot you."

She shot him a disbelieving glance. "Fever must affect your memory. You toddled off to Oxford after that summer, and decided I was of no interest whatsoever."

"Good God, Helena," he protested. "Don't tell me you're holding that against me. I was a stripling of eighteen who suddenly had the whole world before him."

"No." She shook her head. "You know why I can't forgive you."

"Well, it's time you did." He regarded her with exasperation. "It's not my fault you made such a fool of yourself over Crewe."

"You brought him into our lives."

"Damn it, half a dozen fellows stayed with me at Shelton Abbey that summer. You're the one who settled her fancy on the only ne'er-do-well. Every one of the other five turned out to be pillars of society. I know hating me helped you weather the miseries of your marriage, but Crewe has been dead for two years. It's time you placed blame where it belongs. With a blackguard's wiles and an unworldly girl's romantic longings."

She leaped up and stared at West in hurt rage. Right now, if he fainted in front of her, she'd let him lie where he fell.

"You've grown spiteful in Russia." She turned away in a swirl of vermillion skirts. "I'll send a servant to help you back to your bed."

He surged to his feet and caught her arm before she marched out. "Wait, Hel. I don't want to fight."

She struggled to ignore how white he'd gone. "Yet you set yourself to anger me."

"Just tell me I'm not too late."

"You were too late eleven years ago. I won't be your mistress."

He released her and slumped back on the bench in a

quaking heap. "It's worse than that, my cranky Lady Crewe."

"Nothing could be worse than that." She hardly heard what he said. "Let me take you back to the house. You should be in bed."

"You're still offering to join me?" But his question lacked the usual spark.

"It wouldn't do me much good, by the look of you. You don't need excitement. You need a dose of laudanum, and a warm brick wrapped in flannel."

He leaned back and shut his eyes. "Don't fuss, Hel."

Her gaze narrowed. She might care about his well-being—purely as one human to another—but she hadn't forgotten she was annoyed. "As far as I'm concerned, sir, you can curl up in the straw and shrivel away to nothing. But I doubt if Silas wants his best friend giving his last gasp a week before his wedding. It would cast a pall over the celebrations."

West's lips twitched. "So sharp tongued."

"Now aren't you glad that I refused you?"

"Your nagging doesn't scare me."

"It should. No man wants a harridan for a mistress."

He opened his eyes. The green was glassy, and his shivering was worse. Dear heaven, this malady was nasty. "I don't want a harridan for a mistress."

She frowned. He must be delirious. "So what's all that nonsense about missing me?"

He sighed. "Oh, all that is as true as I live."

"Stop teasing, West. It's not funny."

"I'm deadly serious. More serious than I've ever been." His voice was deep and slow, and terrifyingly sincere. "Our timing has always been out of joint, Hel. We were too young when we played at sweethearts. By the time I realized that I was a blockhead to let you go, you'd married Crewe. I waited through your year of mourning to make my move, then damned Liverpool sent me two thousand miles away. But now I'm brooking no more delay. You're here, and I'm here, and no man will say me nay."

She scowled to hide her alarm. For someone on the verge of collapse, he sounded remarkably self-assured. "No man, perhaps. But this woman will never be your mistress."

"I told you I don't want you to be my mistress." That burning gaze didn't waver. "I want you to be my wife."

Before she could respond to that astounding statement, his eyes fluttered shut, and he slid to the ground as if he didn't have a bone in his body.

CHAPTER TWO

*W*est cursed this damned inconvenient fever as he sat beside the fire in Silas's unpretentious drawing room. It was two days since he'd crumpled into a humiliating heap after announcing his intentions to the woman he'd decided to marry. This was his first full evening downstairs.

For nearly a day after blacking out, he hadn't returned to full awareness. When he did, he'd found himself lying in the bedroom he always used at Woodley Park, going back to his earliest boyhood. He'd grown up with the Nash children, and now he hoped to bring that relationship closer, one of family instead of friendship.

At least his dead faint had saved him from hearing Hel's answer. He wasn't optimistic enough to imagine she appreciated his offer. Had ever man set himself to win such a reluctant bride?

The sight of his lady where she sat across the room talking to Fenella Deerham would deter a weaker man. He must have Helena to thank for getting him off the stable floor, but she hadn't come near him since. Caroline and Fenella had called to see him. Even Fenella's hulking lover Anthony Townsend—what a dashed disparate couple that was—had stumped his way up to West's bedroom to wish him a brusque northern-accented recovery.

But Helena's absence had been eloquent. As was the way she kept well out of his way tonight, and avoided addressing him directly.

She did her best to make her rejection clear. Unfortunately for her, he knew her well enough to read beneath the discouraging manner.

Nobody who saw the striking black-haired woman in an emerald gown that set off her olive skin and flashing dark eyes to perfection would discern her abject terror. Nobody but the man who had been first to kiss her, and knew her better than anyone else on earth.

He and Helena had always understood each other. Their long estrangement hadn't changed that.

But that didn't mean he underestimated the obstacles ahead. Crewe, that selfish bastard, had hurt and humiliated her. West had loved the young Helena's generous heart, but that generosity had left her dangerously vulnerable to a rake's lures. Now like a half-broken horse, she shied from another rider.

"They make a right bonny pair, don't they? Sunlight and shadow," a rumbling voice murmured behind him.

West had been so busy staring at Helena, he'd missed Townsend's approach, which was a joke when the fellow was the size of a house.

"Heaven and hell," he said, before he had a chance to censor himself. He'd only met Townsend in the last day or so, and the big, dark man remained something of a mystery.

Townsend gave a grunt of laughter. "If you're calling my Fenella hell, I'll have to shoot you."

West regarded him curiously. Until now, his principal impression of Fenella's unlikely intended was a monumental form and a slight roughness of manner. Now he saw the intelligence gleaming in those deep-set eyes. He recalled that this man had built a huge fortune from nothing.

"You know damn well that's not what I mean."

"Aye, I do. Which is a good thing. I reckon yon Silas won't appreciate a duel on the eve of his wedding."

"Probably not."

Silas and Caro shared a couch, staring at each other as though they couldn't believe their luck. After their rocky courtship, West couldn't blame them for their starry eyes.

Their closeness threw his difficulties with Helena into stark contrast. He didn't begrudge his friends' happiness, but he was painfully envious. When he looked at Silas and Caro, he wanted what they had.

And he wanted it with Helena.

"The lass is making every effort to pretend you don't exist."

"Yes," West said shortly. If a stranger noticed Helena's hostility, that meant old friends like Caro and Silas would, too. Unless they were so wrapped up in each other that the rest of the world could go hang.

"Which I'd take as an encouraging sign."

West's eyebrows rose. "What the devil?"

Townsend released another soft huff of amusement. "She's powerfully interested if she has to try so hard to ignore you."

"She's been furious with me for years," West found himself saying with unexpected honesty. He wasn't a man given to confidences, but something about Anthony Townsend cut through social niceties. It must. In the five years since her husband's death at Waterloo, Fenella had never looked at another man. Yet within mere weeks, Townsend had persuaded her to marry him. The couple planned a quiet ceremony in London before Silas and Caro left for China.

"Aye, I see you're not in her good books."

"I introduced her to Lord Crewe," West said gloomily. "A mistake I sometimes fear I'll pay for until Judgment Day."

"He was a bad 'un, all right. I had the dubious pleasure of making his acquaintance before he broke his neck on that drunken gallop and did the world a favor."

West wasn't quick enough to hide his surprise at the

elevated circles Townsend moved in, and the man shrugged without resentment. "The sprigs of the nobility will stomach my unrefined manners when they want to take advantage of my money."

"Silas always speaks highly of you," West said. "And the rumor is after you saved the government's bacon last year, there's a peerage on the cards."

Townsend's gaze settled on the two women across the room. Lovely, blond-haired Fenella glanced up as if sensing his attention, and the smile she sent him was unmistakably sensual. With a shock that he had no right to feel, West realized that pure, delicate, proper Fenella Deerham was utterly in thrall to her fiancé. They'd share a bed tonight, or he was a Dutchman.

West felt even lonelier. Especially as Helena's current coldness put her bed more out of reach than ever.

"I'd like to give Fenella every honor."

It was West's turn to laugh. "I doubt she gives a fig whether you've got a title or not. She's always been beautiful, but now—"

"She burns like a flame." The burly magnate blushed, and West liked him better for the awkwardness. "Pardon me. I'm not usually given to poetry."

"Congratulations on your good fortune, old man. She's a treasure. In my absence, London's become Cupid's realm."

"Thank you. Now Helena is the last of our widows left to find a husband."

"If I have any say, she won't be a free woman for long."

"So you mean marriage?"

"Of course. She'll make the perfect wife, if I can convince her that I'm not another dissolute rake like Crewe."

"You might have work to do there. Even I've heard the stories about your many conquests."

West shrugged, his attention unwavering on the seemingly oblivious Helena. He didn't feel guilty about his exploits. The women had been willing, the liaisons pleasurable, the partings mostly cordial. He hadn't owed anyone his allegiance—until now.

"I had my moments, but it's time to settle down and set up my nursery." The horror in Townsend's expression made him pause. "What?"

"I hope you didn't say that to Helena. Or it's no wonder your suit doesn't prosper."

Had he wooed her in the stables? He'd been burning up with fever and hardly remembered what he'd said. "Helena knows me too well to fall for sentimental twaddle. And too clever as well."

All the Nashes were dauntingly intelligent. Silas was a famous botanist. Helena devoted her leisure time to higher mathematics, and funding charity schools for bright, but indigent children. Robert put his navigational and engineering gifts into service in the navy. Silas's youngest sister Amy wrote papers on the new agricultural practices.

"No lass is too clever to object to sweet talk from a lad she fancies. I shouldn't have to tell you that. You're the one they call a devil with the ladies."

"Damn it, Hel's different."

Townsend's disapproval melted into disappointment. "I wouldn't be too sure about that. And if her late husband was half the lout I thought him, she's in dire need of tender handling. Kindness might even make her believe you've turned over a new leaf."

West frowned at this man who promised to become a friend. "You don't mince your words."

"I'm no milksop aristocrat, you mean."

West's lips twitched. "I think I meant more than that."

"You can't punch me in the nose with the ladies present," Townsend said placidly. "And you're no fool either. Think about what I said. You'll see I'm right."

"He looks terribly ill," Fenella said, her embroidery lying forgotten on her lap. Helena who wielded a needle with the finesse of a drunken axman, cast an envious glance at the tracery of violets and ivy on cream silk. "It's so romantic that he risked his health to rush to your side."

All thoughts of feminine accomplishments fled Helena's mind, and she stared appalled at her friend. "What on earth did you say?"

Four pairs of curious eyes leveled on them. "Helena, are you all right? What's happened?" Silas asked from across the room.

"Nothing," she muttered. "Go back to gazing into Caro's eyes and whispering romantic inanities."

Caro gave a soft laugh. "She jests at scars who never felt a wound!"

Helena slitted her eyes at her besotted friend and returned her attention to Fenella. This time, she kept her voice low. "What utter balderdash. He's here as Silas's groomsman. They've been friends since childhood."

For such a fairy-like creature, Fenella had a good line in unimpressed looks. "Don't be a nitwit, Hel. He's fond of Silas, but he crossed Europe to see you."

I don't want you to be my mistress. I want you to be my wife.

The words had haunted Helena since West had spoken them in the stables. They were no more acceptable now than they'd been then.

"You're wrong." The last thing she needed was her friends promoting West's asinine courtship. "We don't like each other."

"He likes you." Fenella picked up her tambour and calmly began stitching, as though she discussed the weather and not the prospect of a lifetime of misery for Helena. "He hasn't taken his eyes off you all evening."

"That doesn't mean anything." Helena's hands

clenched on her lap. "Since you've fallen head over heels with Anthony, you see romance everywhere."

"I see it when I look at you and West."

"Then your eyes deceive you. You're living in a fantasy world where each of us finds true love and sails into the sunset clasped to a manly bosom."

"What's wrong with that?"

"Nothing, when it's Caro and Silas, or you and Anthony. I couldn't be happier for you."

It was true, she told herself, even as she stifled an unworthy twinge. She'd never do anything to jeopardize Caro or Fen's happiness, but it was no fun sitting on the sidelines at a party.

As if Fen picked up her shameful envy, she went on. "You'd be happier if you had something new to look forward to. We'll always be friends, but Caro and Silas will be away at least a year, and Anthony and I plan to live in Hampshire with the boys. You'll be all alone in London."

"I have other friends," Helena said, and cringed at how defiant she sounded.

Anyway, it was true. A wealthy widow with a witty tongue could always find company. But since they'd met, she, Caro and Fenella had been inseparable. The other two Dashing Widows understood her in a way that nobody else, except perhaps Silas—and damn him, West—did.

Her hand trembled as she lifted her brandy to her lips. Here on the family estate, strict propriety was relaxed. Even completely tossed out the window. She could have a drink after dinner without raising eyebrows. And while all six people under this roof had been assigned bedrooms, she'd lay good money that neither of the engaged couples slept separately. The only guests sleeping alone tonight were Helena Wade and Vernon Grange. And given a rake's ability to find a bedmate, she wouldn't wager on West remaining lonely.

Stop it, Helena. You don't care who West tups, as long as it's not you.

Sometimes being understood had its drawbacks. Fenella's blue eyes softened with compassion. "You have your schools, and your work, and all the intellectual life of London to occupy you, too."

Oh, dear Lord. At this rate, she'd be sobbing into her brother's best French brandy. She scowled at Fenella. "Don't you dare pity me, Fenella Deerham."

"I want you to be happy."

"I'll be happy." She hoped that Fenella missed the hollow ring beneath her claim. "I have the world at my feet."

"You do."

"Gentlemen vie for my attention."

"Lord Pascal has been most attentive."

"He's a very nice man."

"He is."

Helena's eyes narrowed on her friend. "Stop agreeing with me."

Fenella bit back a smile. "But everything you say is true."

"I've always wanted to travel. Why should Silas and Caro have all the adventures?"

"No reason at all."

"Fenella…" she warned.

Fen shook her head. "There's no pleasing you."

No, there wasn't. And Helena didn't know what in Hades was wrong with her. Life was good. She led a busy and useful existence. She was delighted her friends had found love—she'd all but cornered Caro into agreeing to marry Silas, hadn't she?

She blamed all this blasted love everywhere. It made a woman restless and discontented. Perhaps when she returned to London, she'd do something about turning her agreeable friendship with handsome Lord Pascal into something more. A lover might help to heal the scars left from her marriage.

Pascal was pleasant company. In subtle ways, he'd made it clear that he'd welcome a closer connection. Dear heaven, half London already thought they shared a bed—and the gossip about that had reached as far as Moscow.

She'd take a lover. She'd see Italy and France and Greece. She'd meet interesting people and do exciting things. And she'd ignore the snide little voice that whispered in her ear that she'd do all those wonderful things alone.

It was natural to feel out of sorts with so many

changes around her. She'd find her balance again. And life would become the rich banquet she'd always hoped it could be.

With sudden determination, she emptied her glass and set it on the side table.

But shaky self-confidence dissolved into trepidation when she met West's unwinking green gaze across the opulent room.

CHAPTER THREE

*I*t was late when Helena made her way to her bedroom by the light of a single candle. A headache pounded in her temples, and she was so keyed up, she knew she wouldn't sleep a wink. The familiar house, with its happy childhood memories, settled around her.

Returning to Woodley Park was a bittersweet experience. Inevitably she remembered the lively girl she'd been, and her gentle, intellectual parents, and how close she'd been to her brothers and sister. She also remembered her first fumbling forays into love with West. Except back in those days when every heartbeat had echoed his name, he'd been mere Mr. Vernon Grange.

Compared to that vivacious, warmhearted girl, she felt old and tired and desiccated.

She'd been looking forward to the house party

before Silas's wedding as a chance to spend time with her brother and her friends before everything changed forever. But if tonight indicated what lay ahead, she wished she'd stayed in London. West had made no secret of his interest, and not only had she needed to defend herself against Fenella's matchmaking, Caro tore herself away from Silas long enough to weigh in on the subject, too.

Helena placed the blame on West. Damn him for telling Anthony he wanted to marry her. In the way of lovers, Anthony had told Fenella, who told Caro, who told Silas. Now Helena heartily consigned all her dearest friends to perdition.

When she pushed open the door, her room was aglow with candles. Without surprise, she looked across to the man sitting beside the tall window. Eleven years ago, a snake had poisoned her particular Eden, and his friend was still very much alive to cause trouble.

"Lord West." Her voice was cold.

He bowed his head without standing. She supposed given he'd invaded her room, lesser courtesies hardly mattered. At least he remained fully dressed. "Lady Crewe."

His mockery of her formality was the last straw. "Get out."

"Helena—"

Her hand curled around the doorknob behind her.

She wished she hadn't dismissed her maid for the night before going down to dinner. "You heard me."

He raised his palms in a conciliatory gesture. "I want to talk."

"We can talk. Downstairs. In the full light of day."

"Except you'll go out of your way to avoid me again."

"Doesn't that tell you something?" Her heart raced like a bolting horse. She wanted to say it was with fear, except she wasn't really frightened. At least not that West intended to force his attentions on her.

"It tells me I make you nervous."

"You're making me nervous now. Please go away."

His lips twitched. "You know I mean no harm."

"It depends on your definition of harm. If I shriek for help, Silas and Anthony will hear me."

"They're happily engaged in their own affairs. Pun intended."

"They'd still come to my rescue."

That prompted a quizzical look. "You don't need rescuing."

He stood, and her large, luxurious bedroom turned into a trap. Any confidence that she could bring this unexpected encounter to a speedy end dissolved like sugar in hot water.

"I'll scream."

"You wouldn't be so gauche."

She backed away until she hit the door. "I'm

extremely gauche when it comes to ejecting undesirable intruders from my bedroom."

Except he wasn't undesirable, blast him. Damn all
the love in the air. It sparked reckless ideas in a girl's
head when she found herself alone with an attractive
man after midnight.

West sighed and brushed his hand through his thick
black hair, making it tumble forward over his high
forehead. "Hel, for pity's sake, give me ten minutes, and
if you still feel like a vile monster has cornered you,
I'll go."

Despite herself, she laughed shortly. "You're not a
vile monster, and you know it."

He'd been a beautiful boy and her first love. He'd
grown into a striking man, the perfect picture of the
dark, dashing aristocrat with his chiseled features and
athletic body. Her husband had been another such
classic English gentleman, but mature judgment found
signs of character in West's face that Crewe had lacked.

When Crewe died at twenty-nine, debauchery had
turned him into a wreck. He'd been fat and shaky and sick.
Despite his recent illness, Vernon Grange at thirty was in
the prime of life. He might be pale and too thin. But his
eyes were clear, his jaw was firm, and his mouth expressed
humor and intelligence, not petulant self-indulgence.

His mouth...

"Helena?"

She blinked and realized that she'd drifted off. A

bad idea when she shared a cage with a tiger. West mightn't be as bad as Crewe—the fact that he was alive to pester her testified to that—but he was still dangerous. "I'm sorry. I'm tired."

"Please sit down and listen to me." He gestured toward the bed.

Helena cast him a narrow-eyed look and moved toward the chair on the other side of the window. "As long as there's no marriage nonsense." She blew out her candle and set it on the windowsill between them. "And I'll hold you to the ten minutes."

"You don't give an inch, do you?" He angled his chair so he could watch her. Which wasn't what she wanted. He'd watched her all night, and she had the shredded nerves to prove it.

"Why should I?"

"Because you're missing out on so much."

Her sigh was longsuffering. "I can live very happily without marrying again. I can't see why you'd think to ask me. We don't get along."

"We used to."

"Maybe I should have married you at sixteen," she retorted.

To her disgust, he treated her sarcastic rejoinder as a serious suggestion. "We were too young. I needed to see the world to discover how special you are."

His compliment angered rather than pleased. She made a dismissive gesture. "Don't talk such rubbish.

That might work on your usual witless inamoratas, but I know you too well."

West's regard was steady as he leaned back with every appearance of relaxation. "Knowing someone well is good grounds for marriage."

She shook her head. "Not when I don't like what I know."

"Is that really true?"

"Yes," she said, and didn't believe it herself.

Curse him, why couldn't he lose his temper and march out in a huff, instead of acting like a sensible man? She'd spent eleven years telling herself she despised him. Except that, if she was fair—as she very much didn't want to be—he wasn't quite the thoughtless brute she'd painted him. He took care of his estates, and he could sound intelligent when he felt like it. His negotiation skills had gained international respect. When the government sent him to Russia to sort out that diplomatic mess, it wasn't the first time they'd turned to him for help.

West didn't take offense at her rudeness. Of course he didn't. He knew she didn't hate him, whatever self-serving lies she told. "That's a pity when we have so much in common. Our childhoods, our friendships, our love of horses."

"It doesn't matter, West. I'm not interested in marrying again. Even if I was, I'd never choose another man who I couldn't trust to stay in my bed."

His tone hardened, and he straightened in his chair. "I haven't had a mistress in more than a year."

"Making do with casual encounters, are you?" she asked, while the more generous side of her nature stood appalled at how crabbed and snide she sounded. Crewe had changed her so powerfully, and in ways that she hated, but couldn't seem to overcome.

He shook his head. "You've become so bitter, Hel. I hate to see it."

The fact that he was right didn't mean she had to agree. She shrugged. "Do you blame me?"

"Crewe has been dead two years. Your best revenge is to rise above his sins against you and lead a fulfilled life."

She loathed that a man she wanted to deride as a self-centered lightweight was so perceptive. "As your wife?"

He surged to his feet and moved to stand over her, bracing his elegant hands on the chair arms. "Yes, if you like. But I'd give my right arm to see you experience some real happiness. I don't believe you've had one moment of unsullied joy since you married that toad."

Helena pressed back against the chair's brocade upholstery and fought to control angry, anguished tears. She wanted to protest that she was happy when she and Artemis galloped fit to outrun the world. But that would only make her sound more pitiable.

"Stop it," she said in a choked voice.

He grabbed her shoulders in adamant hands. "I'd like to shake some sense into you."

His touch made her stiffen. "How irresistible that makes the idea of marrying you," she forced through lips that threatened to tremble.

She'd survived the last ten years by pretending nothing could hurt her. Be damned if she'd cry in front of West.

He sighed, and the anger drained from his face. Lifting his hands, he stepped back with a gesture of apology. "I'm sorry, Hel. I swore I'd be civilized. But I care too much."

She was seriously rattled now. If his emotions were engaged, it would be almost impossible to discourage his pursuit. She tried to speak lightly, but her voice emerged high and unnatural. "You're feeling nostalgic because we're back in old haunts."

"No."

He sounded so sure. As another wave of fear rippled through her, she raised her chin. "You've had your ten minutes."

His smile was wry. "Damn me, so I have."

Crewe hadn't possessed an ounce of self-awareness. West's self-mockery reminded her again that he was a better man than her late husband. "So good night."

Self-aware West might be. Malleable he was not. He drew himself up and stared at her with a green-eyed glint she didn't trust. "I haven't got to what I want to talk about."

"I won't marry you."

"That wasn't it."

She frowned, curious despite herself. "Wasn't it?"

"No." He reached for her hand and pulled her up—and far too close. "You asked about the women in my life."

"Actually I didn't. You told me that of late, you've avoided steady liaisons."

"Any liaisons at all."

She surveyed him cynically, although the rational part of her brain squeaked in protest that she shouldn't care who shared his bed. And worse, interest would encourage his delusions that she was more than a childhood friend. "Even in Russia?"

"Even in Russia. By God, those nights were cold."

"I assume you mean your uncharacteristic chastity as some sort of compliment." Her voice sharpened. "Well, I don't want it."

He shrugged. "It's not for you to decide." The glint in his eyes changed to determination. "When there's only one woman I want, it seems shabby to waste my time with substitutes."

"Then you'll be sleeping alone for a long time," she snapped. Because despite everything she knew about rakes, including that they lied—and who was to say he'd been faithful during those chilly St. Petersburg nights?—something inside her melted to think he'd turned away armies of women for her sake.

Which proved she wasn't much smarter than the

wide-eyed virgin who had fallen so disastrously under Lord Crewe's spell.

"That's what I'm here to talk about." Before she could repeat that she'd never marry him, he rushed on. "An affair. I want an affair."

A vibrating silence crashed down. Then Helena burst out laughing. "You're persistent. I'll give you that."

His grip on her hand firmed. "Hear me out."

"Another ten minutes?"

"You have other plans for tonight?"

His audacity made her laugh again. He was impossible. "Oh, to Hades with you. All right. I'm listening. You told me in the stables you don't want a mistress."

Another charming, self-deprecating smile. "I didn't, until I entered this bower of hearts and flowers. You and I are de trop amongst all the billing and cooing."

"So because we're at loose end, we should jump into bed?"

"I've bedded women for less valid reasons."

She gasped at his impudence. "Perhaps now and again, you should try a good book instead."

"That's what you do—and it's left you a bundle of nerves and frustration." He tugged on her hand, but she resisted his attempt to bring her closer. "Come on, Hel. I know you. I know the passion simmering under all those thorns. Unless you've been unbelievably discreet, you haven't taken a lover since Crewe broke his neck. Caro told me about you and Pascal. Poor sap's hanging out for an encouraging word, but he's not getting one. I know how he feels."

Annoyance flattened her lips. "Caro's a telltale."

"She doesn't like to see me suffer." He paused. "Surely you want to revisit the pleasures of the flesh— two years of chastity must chafe."

For a shocked moment, she stared at him. Then the ludicrous situation struck her with full force. She jerked away and collapsed back into her chair, laughing.

"Helena?" West asked when she didn't stop. "What the devil is the matter?"

"I can't—" she spluttered and set off on another peal of giggles. To think, this was the man who claimed to understand her. Yet everything he said was wrong, wrong, wrong.

He went down on his haunches and grabbed her shoulders. Genuine concern darkened his expression. "Helena, damn well calm down."

She sucked in a breath, feeling better for the good laugh, however bitter its cause.

And because she felt better, she admitted the unvarnished truth. "There were no pleasures of the flesh in my marriage. Crewe was as useless with a woman as he was with everything else."

CHAPTER FOUR

*W*est had led a full and exciting life. He'd traveled. He'd indulged his sensual appetites, some might say to a fault. He'd experienced human nature in all its rich variety. At thirty, very little surprised him anymore.

Helena's confession left him speechless. And appalled.

That this glorious creature had never experienced sexual pleasure was too cruel to be borne. His liking for her drunken brute of a husband hadn't much outlasted that ill-fated visit to Shelton Abbey when Crewe met his bride. But this went beyond all the evil he already knew of Gerald Wade.

"I won't have you feeling sorry for me," she snarled, staring up at him like a deer surrounded by hounds. Except even when she left herself vulnerable, Helena stayed fierce.

Not a deer. A lioness.

West studied her taut, troubled features, and did the only thing he could.

He kissed her.

Her confession called for gentleness. Kindness. Reassurance. But her fire had always lured him. The knowledge that her fire had never had a chance to blaze into magnificent conflagration made him seethe.

And crave.

So when he dragged her up from the chair into his arms, his touch was ruthless. The lips he pressed to hers were hungry, and made no concession to what remained an essential innocence.

She cried out in protest, and her hands clenched on his arms. When he'd caught her, she'd been too startled to resist. Now she went as rigid as a block of wood.

Not as rigid as he was. He'd wanted Helena for months. Years. Touching her, he went up in flames. As volatile as the idealistic, untried boy he'd once been.

More. Now he was a man. His desire was a man's desire.

Her mouth was unresponsive. But her smoky scent, familiar yet new, made his head swim. She fitted against him, created for his pleasure. She was a tall, slender woman, and that lissome body drove him mad.

Drowning in heat, he took too long to realize that she was pounding on his shoulders. "What the devil?" he gasped, wrenching free.

Since her marriage, she'd masked her ardent soul

beneath intellectual detachment. Now she was incandescent with emotion. Unfortunately the emotion wasn't passion. Rage set her black eyes glittering.

Her defiance only made him burn to kiss her again. Once, he'd feared that Crewe's betrayals might crush her tempestuous soul.

Not in a million years.

"I begin to believe you," he said in a drawl meant to stoke her fury. He didn't want her taking refuge in defensive coolness. "Crewe didn't teach you much about kissing. You were better at this when you were sixteen."

Temper flared in Helena's eyes like an exploding star. "I don't want pity kisses," she snapped. "You will not laugh at me."

"Idiot girl," he said with fond impatience, and swept her up, blatantly pressing her against him. "Does that feel like pity?"

"You—" she stammered, drawing back. Astonishment chased her anger away.

"Yes, I want you." He answered the unfinished question. "I've always wanted you. Even when you were another man's wife."

Wonderingly she studied him. His candor didn't seem to have offended her, which was a surprise. "I had no idea."

"You've been locked away from life." His grip on her arms tightened. "Let me show you what you've missed."

When her dark gaze settled on his mouth, something sparked in those starry depths. Arousal jolted him. And the beginnings of hope.

"What if I don't like it?"

"I'll stop." He hoped to Hades he wasn't lying.

"I'm not sure I trust you."

"If you shriek your head off, someone will save you."

Ironic amusement curled her lips. "You're convinced you can kiss any objections away, aren't you?"

He shrugged. "I've had no complaints."

She subjected him to the comprehensive inspection she'd give a horse before she bought it. "I feel...I feel that my education is lacking. Especially since Caro and Fen..."

"Have found their own satisfaction?"

"Yes." To stop him gathering her closer, she flattened her hand on his chest. "If we do this..."

"If?" *If* was better than an outright refusal any day. Triumph beat inside him like a thousand wings. He'd intrigued her—and Helena followed where her curiosity led.

"If we do this, I set the pace. After you've kissed me, I decide whether we proceed."

A grunt of incredulous laughter escaped him. "You're still a blasted managing wench. Do you want me to sign a contract? In triplicate? In blood?"

His sarcasm didn't amuse her. "Your word is sufficient."

"Damn it, Hel. I'm asking for a few days of fun, not hiring an architect to build me a new townhouse." Actually he intended much more than a brief affair, but however heady her nearness, he hadn't lost his grip on strategy.

His levity earned him a disapproving glance. "There's more."

He sighed and settled his hands at her supple waist. "Of course there is."

"You won't tell anybody."

"Not even Silas?"

"Silas in particular. If you tell Silas, he'll tell Caro. Then she'll tell Fen. I don't want any misguided, if well-meant matchmaking. In public, we still act like acquaintances."

West arched his eyebrows. "When you're wandering around in a blissful daze, that will be difficult."

This time she did push away. He didn't try to stop her. Right now, she wasn't going anywhere.

"I hate to puncture your confidence, but it's possible there won't be any bliss." She paced as she spoke. Hers was a restless soul, always had been.

He frowned as he watched her move. Those long legs ate up the carpet, and everything about her expressed energy and purpose. She was the most exciting woman he'd ever known. "I'm not a brute like Crewe."

The smile she cast him in passing was almost fond. "I know you're not."

He gaped at her in shock. "What did you say?"

She came to rest near the bed and curled her hand around one of the carved posts. He gulped for air. The action was a little too suggestive for his sanity. And the pity of it was she had no clue.

As if ensuring he understood, she spoke very clearly. "I said you're a better man than my late, unlamented spouse. Why else are we having this conversation?"

He frowned, struggling through the steam in his brain to make sense of this momentous change. "You always said we were cut from the same cloth."

"Yes, well, I was hurt and angry. Just now, when I asked you to stop kissing me, you did. Crewe would have rushed on to find his swinish satisfaction."

Did she know how much she betrayed about her marriage? "Helena…"

She glowered. "I told you not to feel sorry for me. When I decided I wouldn't share him with his whores, I started sleeping with a pistol under my pillow. You might recall his *hunting* accident, back in 1811. The one that didn't kill him, but left him with his arm in a sling."

"You?" What a woman she was. He wanted to give three cheers.

Her lips curled in bloodthirsty self-satisfaction. "After that, he took me seriously."

"The worm. I'll make it up to you."

She laughed without amusement. "You don't have

to heal every hurt, West, although it's sweet to think the chivalrous boy still lurks under that worldly hide."

He winced at the word "sweet." Between falling at her feet like a poltroon and completely misinterpreting her past, he was making a damned fool of himself. Something about Helena undermined arrogance. Worse, he wanted to protect and cherish her.

How she'd scoff if he admitted that.

"I always wished you well."

Her memorable features softened into true beauty. "I'm sorry it's taken so long to forgive you."

West released a breath that he felt he'd held for years. Her resentment had always niggled like a stone in his shoe. Whatever else tonight brought, he was damned grateful that at last they reached an understanding.

"At least you have." When he made to close in on her, she waved her hand to keep him at a distance.

"I need to say this before we go on. Crewe always said I'm…unnatural. It was my fault that he had to find ease elsewhere."

That slimy, vicious sod. "That's self-serving spite."

"He could be spiteful. But…" She looked away toward the window. "Perhaps he was right, and I'm incapable of a woman's response."

Helena incapable of desire? He'd never heard such claptrap. "You forget I've held you in my arms."

"That was a long time ago." Still she avoided his

eyes. These confidences tested her pride. "And we never…"

"You were only sixteen, and my best friend's sister. I have a small measure of honor."

"Silas would have killed you."

"Slowly and painfully. And then he'd put my body through a mincer." West ran his hand through his hair. "Helena, there's absolutely nothing wrong with you, apart from a capacity to hold a grudge."

"I hope you're right."

He made another move.

Again she gestured him back. "I haven't finished."

With a theatrical sigh, he rolled his eyes. "I was wrong. This is worse than contracting to build a new townhouse."

"If…if this arrangement goes ahead, I reserve the right to end it."

"Once you've satisfied curiosity?" Sourness tinged his question. "I don't feel like an architect anymore. I feel like the subject of a scientific experiment."

She didn't smile. "You don't have to agree."

"Yes, I do." Not only because he wanted her more than he'd wanted anything else in his life. After tonight's revelations, he had the strangest feeling that she needed him. Even if she didn't recognize it, and would never admit it if she did.

"Because you've got something to prove?"

He was canny enough not to confide his thoughts. "Maybe."

"And you're not to mention marriage."

West swept a finger across his lips to indicate they were forever sealed. "No M words."

"I mean it."

She didn't trust his easy cooperation. A smart girl, his Helena. But in this, he was at least one step ahead of her. She'd forgotten his reputation as a negotiator. Tonight, her concessions exceeded his most extravagant hopes. From here, he could forge ahead and win the war.

Helena Wade didn't know it yet, but he had her exactly where he wished.

As if taking an oath, he raised his hand. "For the duration of our stay at Woodley Park, I foreswear all mention of marriage, wedding, vicar, wife, husband, nuptials, proposals, and all similar and related terms, so help me, God."

"You're looking too pleased with yourself, West." Her tone was suspicious. "I don't like it."

"I'm about to kiss a lovely woman." He strove for a guileless expression. It didn't come naturally. "Why shouldn't I be happy?"

"I know you. You're as cunning as a rat."

By God, she was a delight. Despite his maneuvering, she wasn't near defeated. The dance would go on, and if he didn't concentrate on every step, he'd stumble in a heap. This edgy wooing proved devilish entertaining. The elusive Lady Crewe was a quarry worth the pursuit. "Hardly flattering."

"But accurate." Her regard remained wary. "You've been a slippery customer since you were in your cradle."

He spread his hands. "I agree to everything you ask."

"That's what worries me."

"Enough talk." This time he ignored the message of her raised hand and stepped close enough to catch her smoky scent. "If I don't kiss you in the next second, I'll explode."

She searched his face for signs of deceit. "You're up to something. I know it."

He caught the fluttering hands that betrayed how flustered she was. "No more, Helena. It's time to lay down your guns and surrender. Close your eyes and pucker up."

"Oh, very well, if I must," she said, as though fronting up to a punishment.

But she tilted her face with breathtaking sweetness, and when he drew her into his arms, she was soft and warm and pliant.

CHAPTER FIVE

*H*ow strange to be in West's arms again. Fleetingly Helena became once more the innocent girl who had been so mad for him.

Except his easy strength was new, and the confidence. This was a man who knew how to touch a woman. Whereas she felt tremulous and untried, as if those poisonous years with Crewe had never existed.

Slowly she ran her palms up his chest, feeling the heat of his skin through his shirt. The mature West was an altogether more substantial figure than his younger self. The body under her hands was firm with muscle, even if he was too thin after his illness.

Remembering how mere days ago, he'd been racked with fever prompted her to steal this chance. In recent years, her only physical pleasure had been a good gallop on a fine horse—and little enough of that. What a tragic waste. West was right. Crewe might be in the grave, but still he blighted her life.

Once she'd loved kissing. West and she had whiled away a whole summer with kisses. Even Crewe had known how to kiss her into a lather of desire, when he could be bothered. It was what came after kissing that left her cringing with frustration and shame.

Tonight she couldn't bear to be that pathetic creature.

"What's wrong?" West whispered.

Startled, she emerged from the unhappy past to find the man of the present observing her with concern. His hands sat loosely at her waist.

Once she gave her consent, she'd expected him to leap on her. His kiss had caught her unprepared. Unprepared and unafraid. The lack of fear had convinced her that despite years of pique, at some instinctual level, she still trusted her first love.

"Why do you ask?"

His tender expression twisted her heart. Even in courtship, Crewe had never given her a scrap of tenderness. To her adolescent self, that had seemed thrilling proof of overmastering passion. Today's Helena knew better.

"Because you were as supple as a willow wand, and now you're all tight and wary again."

To her surprise, she responded honestly. Tonight was unprecedented in so many ways, not least because she abandoned all defenses. Or they abandoned her. "I'm nervous."

More breathtaking tenderness. "So am I."

She frowned her disbelief. "Don't play games, West."

"You challenged me to show you pleasure. Good God, it's more responsibility than the government laid on my shoulders when I went to Russia. Then I only had to worry about the fate of empires."

Something coiled and suspicious inside Helena loosened as she laughed. "You're absurd."

He cupped the side of her face. "And you're lovely."

The tightness returned. "No, I'm not. My nose is too big."

It was West's turn to laugh. "I love your nose. I always have. It has such character. A woman so imperious would look silly with a little button nose. You're a queen, Helena, not a pretty little poppet."

When he kissed her long blade of a nose, she shifted uncomfortably. Crewe had left her mistrusting everything about herself, including her looks. Now she hated how she yearned for more of West's praise. "You don't have to—"

"Give you compliments? I do, if you're mad enough to underestimate your attractions."

She snorted. "Overdoing it, West."

He grabbed her hand and pressed it over his pounding heart. "Feel that?"

Wide-eyed Helena stared at him. "For me?"

"For you."

Without stopping to second-guess herself, she rose on her toes—West was one of the few men she knew tall enough to make her feel small and feminine—and pressed her lips to his.

Her boldness startled him, and he jerked away. "Helena, are you sure?"

Yes, definitely a better man than her louse of a husband. She hooked her hands over his broad shoulders. "No."

This time when she kissed him, she leaned closer, nipping at his lower lip until he let her in. When his arms lashed around her and his mouth opened over hers, triumph filled her.

After all this time, she'd expected to feel more tentative, but this was like coming home after a long, difficult journey. A voluptuous sigh escaped, and she parted her lips to allow him access. His tongue thrust into her mouth, and she met him eagerly.

Closing her eyes, she gave herself up to a sizzling universe of sensation. West's scent was richer and more potent than she remembered, and he tasted so delicious. Heat swept through her with swift and irresistible force. A powerful pulse set up in the base of her belly.

Helena moaned against his seeking lips, as his hands roamed up and down her back. Only when her bodice sagged did she realize he touched her with intent.

She wasn't hypocrite enough to protest. At last

blood flowed through her veins. For years, she'd lived in ice.

With frantic hands, she pushed the coat and waist-coat from his shoulders, and tore at his neck cloth until his soft, white shirt fell open. Greedily her palms danced across the planes of his chest.

When he stepped back, she growled deep in her throat. Eyes glittering with purpose, he wrenched her blue silk bodice down.

"West..." she gasped, hands flying up to cover her breasts.

He caught her wrists and lowered them to her sides. "I've wanted this since we hid behind the stables and kissed each other to insanity." His voice was hoarse with desire.

Looking back, she realized how careful he'd been with her. West might act the rake, but in essence, he was a good man. And recognizing that, she relaxed her arms in silent compliance. He released her wrists and cupped her breasts in his large hands. She shivered as he flicked his thumbs over her nipples, teasing them to dark pink points.

"So lovely," he murmured, and closed his lips over one yearning peak. She started. And started again when his tongue rasped over her. Her knees turned to water, and unsteady hands clutched his shoulders.

"You're...you're tormenting me."

His soft laugh tickled her skin, before he directed his attention to her other breast. A nip made her cry out and press closer. That hot, skillful mouth set her blood singing.

She thrust her hips forward, wantonly presenting herself. One hand curled into his shoulder, while the other tangled in his thick, warm hair. She wriggled, trying to relieve that insistent, thunderous throb between her legs.

Only when she was pulling his hair and panting did he raise his head. His eyes were heavy and dark, and that expressive mouth was fuller than usual.

"Let me have you." The arm around her waist tensed in demand, but still she didn't feel threatened. "Tonight."

Tonight? In confusion, she shook her head. How could he ask her to make decisions when every touch threatened to incinerate her?

Disappointment flooded his eyes, and he reluctantly pulled away. "Damn, Hel, I'm sorry."

"No." Eager hands snatched at his arms.

Puzzled he stared at her. "No?"

"No." Licking her lips, she tasted West. "No, don't go."

He straightened. "So really it's yes?"

West was always presented *comme il faut*, with never a hair out of place. No wonder the government sent him abroad as England's perfect gentleman. Now he looked ferocious and on edge, a thousand miles from the nonpareil who graced London's drawing rooms. The thick black hair was mussed. His creased shirt hung loose about his narrow hips. Stubble darkened his jaw, potent reminder of his masculinity.

"For God's sake, Hel," he burst out when she didn't speak. "You must know you're safe with me. Not every man's a bastard like Crewe."

Not even the mention of her vile husband pierced the spell falling over her. "You've grown up devilish handsome, you know, West," she said slowly. "I've never taken the time to appreciate you properly."

To her delight, this world-weary libertine blushed a painful red. "What flummery."

An instinct she hesitated to trust after the debacle with Crewe insisted that this time she wouldn't end in a humiliated huddle. This time she chose a lover worthy of the name. After tonight, she'd understand the glow that surrounded Fen and Caro.

Years of tension flowed away, leaving behind pure desire. She must look revoltingly dreamy. Like West, she'd waited so long for this moment.

"Take me to bed."

West must be dreaming. Had he fallen asleep waiting for Helena? Surely she hadn't just invited him to tup her.

"West?"

No dream then. Thank you, God. He'd spent his

entire adult life wanting her. Now lovely, unattainable Helena was here, warm, willing, and welcoming.

"I was planning the many ways I mean to pleasure you."

"Perhaps you should stick to the basics." Uncertainty dimmed her eyes. "Remember I'm out of practice."

She was more than out of practice—she was a rank beginner. Crewe must have gone at his wife completely ham-fisted. West wanted to break the bastard's neck all over again.

"A woman who rides a horse like you do will have no trouble with another sort of riding."

Her low, sultry chuckle made him as hard as a fence post. Even as a girl, she'd had this siren's voice, husky, alluring, suggestive.

He caught her by the hips and kissed her, poignantly aware that despite nine years of marriage, she was in essence still virginal. Difficult to remember when she curled against him and opened her mouth. Impossible when her tongue flickered around his in a hectic dance that threatened to blow his head off.

She wrenched away and glared at him, all fire and arrogance. "Don't you dare."

"What—"

"You're feeling sorry for me again."

"Damn it, Helena, I'm trying to be considerate."

"Don't," she growled. "If Crewe couldn't break me, nothing can."

What a damned sapskull he was. He did her an injustice. Tonight she'd revealed her vulnerability, and he'd let that blind him to her resilience. She deserved everything he could give. More, she thrived on someone matching her. He only had to recall those impudent letters to recognize that. "I don't want to break you. I want to make you whole."

Her eyes narrowed. "I am whole. You know me, West. I'm no shrinking violet."

This woman threw herself over towering fences on horses most men would hesitate to mount. She always rode at the front of the pack. If he wanted to keep up with her, he must play the game to the best of his ability.

The challenge fired his blood.

He nodded. "Very well. No concessions for the weaker opponent."

She made a dismissive sound. "I'm not your inferior."

"You most certainly are not." With sudden urgency, he wrenched his shirt over his head and flung it into the corner. "But remember when you're hot and panting and begging for mercy, that you asked for this."

A brief laugh. "I'd like to see that."

So, by the devil, would he. His confidence surged when her covetous gaze fastened on his bare chest. She licked her lips again. Satan and all his minions, every time she did that, he nearly lost himself.

He toed off his shoes and reached for his trousers.

Predictably her lustful expression made his cock swell. Before he could accept her unspoken invitation, she tugged the skirts of her blue gown. The sibilant whisper when it crumpled to the ground was one of the most evocative sounds he'd ever heard.

"There's a heaven, and I'm in it," he murmured. It was his turn to devour her with his eyes. "You still hold a lot of surprises, Helena."

Her bold front was touchingly unconvincing. "I like wearing pretty things."

"The pleasure is all mine." He stepped back to take in Helena's undergarments. Red rosebuds trailed with seeming artlessness across filmy lawn.

With a very un-Helena-like fumble, she untied her petticoat. It slithered down with more of that damned rustling. Her shift offered ghost glimpses of pearled pink nipples and the dark hair concealing her sex. A satin corset embroidered with more roses slanted across her body where he'd tugged it awry. West's fingers curled at his sides at the prospect of tracing the twining roses, then discovering her smooth olive skin beneath.

Scarlet garters held up sheer, white stockings, and the ribbons on her satin slippers, blue to match her dress, tied around her neat ankles. In all his days, he'd never seen such a pretty picture.

"You naughty girl." His gaze sharpened as heat speared him. "You're not wearing drawers."

"Sometimes, I…I don't." The stammer wasn't like her either. "I take it you approve."

"I'm out of my bloody mind with approval. It's a good thing I never knew what was under those dauntingly stylish gowns, or you'd have found yourself compromised well before this. It was hard enough keeping my hands off you anyway."

She looked gratifyingly intrigued. "Really?"

"Yes, really," he said, as though he swore his life away. He drew a hairpin from the mass of black hair coiled at her nape. "With your hair like this, you remind me of a renaissance princess."

Her mouth, red with kisses, quirked with familiar, endearing humor. "Lucretia Borgia?"

"Someone a little less murderous." He removed two more pins. A silky skein of black snaked down across her shoulder. Delicately he lifted it and brought it to his lips, breathing deep. Her rich scent flooded his senses. Smoky. Female. Unforgettable. So true to the woman she was.

Wonderingly she studied him. "You're not—"

He smoothed the lock back, admiring its dense blackness against her skin. "I'm not what?"

"You're not in a hurry."

How criminally careless Crewe had been with her. "It doesn't signal lack of appetite."

Her gaze lowered to the bulge in his trousers. "It's… nice. As though you're taking time to enjoy each flavor, not just bolting the meal down."

West laughed and kissed her. Through the busy years, and lovers who had meant far too little, as he now recognized with regret, he'd never forgotten Helena. She was endlessly fascinating, extraordinary. Salty and satisfying, where sugar palled.

She responded with pleasing swiftness, and his brief kiss turned into something long and profound. He buried his hands in her hair. When he drew away, it tumbled loose around her slender shoulders.

He nibbled a path down her neck, feeling her shiver, as he disposed of corset and shift. At last he set his hands on her naked body. "You're beautiful."

She raised her chin and faced him proudly. Tall. Slender. Long-legged. Graceful as a young goddess. "I'm glad you like me."

"I've always liked you." His smile was wry. "Haven't you worked that out yet?"

She didn't answer. That was all right. Soon she'd admit her fondness for him.

While West took off his trousers, Helena perched on the bed to remove slippers and stockings. The sight of her bare calves and feet enthralled him. Odd how random, seemingly insignificant moments kept catching him on the raw.

Tomorrow he'd ponder reasons. Right now, Helena awaited. He cast away the last of his clothing and strode toward the lovely woman, watching wide-eyed from the luxurious bed.

CHAPTER SIX

$\mathcal{H}$elena gulped for air and curled her hands into the sheets beneath her. The opulent room turned suffocating. And tiny.

While West seemed terrifyingly…large.

"Dear heaven…" she croaked from a mouth that felt drier than a desert. She couldn't look away from the stiff column of flesh rising between his legs.

West laughed. "Hel, don't tell me you've never seen a naked man before."

She couldn't mistake his affectionate amusement. The traitorous warmth in her chest became harder to deny. She licked parched lips and managed to squeak out, "Crewe didn't look like you."

West's eyebrows rose. "I assure you I'm perfectly normal. Well, apart from the damned fever I picked up in the Crimea, but that hasn't changed my basic anatomy."

"I'm going to faint," she said in a thready voice.

"Never. Not my stalwart Helena."

How she wished she shared his confidence. Although sparking excitement underlay her trepidation. Excitement and curiosity. And something that could be need.

Despite her best efforts, the hand she stretched toward him trembled. "Show me."

He covered the distance in a single stride and caught her in his arms. As he lowered her to the bed, his touch swept away all misgivings.

He kissed her ravenously and set out to explore her body, learning every line and hollow. When his fingers trailed between her legs, her thighs fell open. What point playing coy when she ached with desire?

A sound of satisfaction emerged from his throat as he bent to take her nipple between his lips. Sensation assaulted her from two directions at once, and every muscle contracted in response. Nothing Crewe had done could compare to these shuddering reactions.

And West had barely started.

He stroked her cleft and lingered on a sensitive place that sent lightning streaking through her. She whimpered as a liquid surge greeted his daring caresses. Her heart hammered against her ribs, as if it fought to break free.

The tension rose higher and higher while he tormented that small, secret pearl. She squirmed. The pleasure sharpened until it approached pain. She gasped when he slid one long finger into her, adding to the giddy mix.

"Let it happen, Hel." He raised his head from her breast and stared at her. "Don't fight me."

She gasped as her body stretched to accept two seeking fingers. "Fight you?" She couldn't contain an unsteady laugh. "I'm positively begging."

Something flashed in his eyes that struck her as important. If only she could read it. "You're pure gold. You always have been."

He curled his fingers inside her and stroked a place that set her quaking. Yet still what she wanted remained out of reach.

It had been like this with Crewe. He'd take her so far, then while he found release, she'd stay teetering on the brink. She dug her fingernails into West's arms in a silent plea not to leave her behind.

"It won't work," she gasped. "I think it's going to, then—"

He kissed her, and the touch of his lips soothed the demons. "Trust me."

"Crewe was right. There's something wrong with me."

"Damn it, there's nothing wrong with you, except the man you chose to marry."

West kissed her again, until she forsook self-doubt and yielded. His fingers moved in and out of her with a hard, regular rhythm that made her shake. Each time he withdrew, the heel of his hand pressed on her mound and fire shot through her. Craving spiraled tighter and tighter, until surely she must snap into pieces.

Fulfillment still hovered too far off. As release evaded her, stinging tears seeped from her eyes. She couldn't do it. Even with West, even wanting him so desperately.

"Curse you, you'll get there," he snarled, urgency roughening his voice. He changed the angle of his caresses and lowered his head to the curve between her neck and shoulder.

As he bit down hard, pain and pleasure collided in a fiery crash. Helena cried out in wonder. The world shattered around her, and she crossed the barrier into glory.

Free. She was finally free. And swooping and dipping and rolling among the stars. The view from paradise was extraordinary. As her blood lit to unquenchable fire, she shivered and squirmed. And when she wafted down from that blazing peak, even the embers were beautiful.

After a long time, she opened dazzled eyes to see West beside her, leaning on his elbow. A lazy smile hovered around his lips.

She rose to kiss him with all the poignant gratitude she felt.

He looked startled. "What was that for?"

"Thank you."

"No, thank *you.*"

She struggled for some way to describe the experience. "That was even better than a good gallop."

He burst out laughing and flopped back onto the sheets. "Hel, you're priceless."

Helena frowned, although she felt too marvelous for genuine displeasure. For years, she'd closed more and more of herself away, until a hard little ball of hurt and hate and self-pity lodged in her chest instead of a heart. Those miraculous moments when West had set her flying let her breathe for the first time since she was a carefree girl. "And you're a lunatic."

His green eyes glittered as he sucked in an unsteady breath. "No argument there." Another breath. "Actually that counts as high praise from horse-mad Helena Nash."

He'd used her maiden name. As if they returned to those sweet days when she'd been in his thrall. Before she'd decided dark, dangerous Lord Crewe was the most exciting man she'd ever met.

How tragically wrong she'd been.

"It was a compliment," she said.

"I'm sure." His tone was dry.

He rose above her and kissed her with a serious intent that his tone belied. His legs tangled with hers, and his hips pressed her into the mattress with sensual purpose. She shifted and felt his powerful hardness against her belly. Interest sparked anew, although surely she'd received her measure of delight.

When he stroked her slick cleft, she raised her

knees. She didn't expect to experience more of that sublime pleasure, but she didn't mind. She wanted West inside her. She wanted to offer him a share of the delight he'd given her.

His back tensed under her hands, then with a smoothness she hardly believed, he thrust inside her.

"West," she gasped in shock, opening her eyes wide. He looked powerful and intent—and strained. At last she saw how the leisured seduction had tested his control.

He rested on his elbows and looked down at her. "Am I hurting you?"

Helena wriggled, feeling him settle inside her, hard and purposeful. "No."

"Not too big?"

A smile tugged at her lips. How flustered she'd been. How silly. Right now, she felt magnificently full, as though he laid claim to every inch. "Perfect."

He kissed her again. After they'd married, Crewe hadn't been interested in much beyond his own relief. He hadn't wasted time on kissing.

She'd missed out.

"Hold on."

With uncharacteristic obedience, she clutched West's broad shoulders. His skin was hot and satiny against hers. His masculine musk imbued every breath she took. Instinctively she tightened.

His eyes darkened, and a muscle flickered in his hard cheek. "Merciful God."

She tugged at the damp strands of hair at his nape. "Good?"

"Damn good."

This time she contracted on purpose, and exulted in his shudder. Giving West pleasure was a pleasure. Perhaps he hadn't been quite as unselfish with her as she'd credited. She arched up to bite his neck, and he shuddered again.

"You'll kill me before you're done," he grated out.

"At least you'll die smiling."

Her eyelids fluttered in bliss at the slow glide away. When he slid inside again, she rose to meet him, bringing him deeper.

Helena's wordless encouragement broke some last bastion of his will. He began to move with inexorable purpose. She thrilled to his male power. His breath escaped in soft grunts, and his muscles turned hard and hot as granite under a noonday sun.

With luxuriant enjoyment, she ran her hands down his long back to his firm buttocks. How she loved West's possession. She felt like the only woman in the world.

Astonishingly, as he pursued that relentless rhythm, a now familiar response fermented in the pit of her stomach. The sensation spread, flooding her with heat. By the time his control frayed, she trembled on the verge.

He surged up hard and fast. The tendons on his

neck stood out in relief. His grip on her hips turned unyielding. On a great groan, he plunged one last time.

She dived into the fire, closing hard around him. This response was deeper and purer than the first time. As she crashed out of the mundane world into the brilliance of the sun, West stayed with her. Her fingernails scored his shoulders, and she arched toward him in shaking, incoherent delight.

"Damn it, Hel," he bit out.

As she quivered in helpless rapture, he held her beneath him. Then with another rasping groan, he wrenched out, and pumped his seed onto her naked belly.

CHAPTER SEVEN

*W*est rolled off Helena and slumped facedown in the tangled sheets. He gasped for air. She'd been the answer to a dream— better than a dream. Damn it, he'd come so close to spilling himself inside her. He'd never taken the act right to the edge like that before. Withdrawing had nearly killed him.

The temptation of Helena.

"West?" she asked in a threadbare voice beside him.

"Nggrrr," he managed. If she expected a sensible conversation after that thunderous ride, she overestimated his stamina.

"West, talk to me."

God help him, the woman really wanted a chat. When at last he managed to shift, he was surprised he didn't creak. He'd given her everything he had. He never wanted to move again.

Exhaustion weighted his limbs, but the need to care for her forced him from the bed. He stoked the fire before crossing to the washstand. The water in the jug was still blessedly warm. He cleaned himself off, then splashed fresh water into the bowl, collected a cloth, and returned to the bed.

Helena lay splayed against the pillows like a naked odalisque. In recent years, she'd always been elegant and self-possessed. Seeing her like this, disheveled, flushed with passion, thick black hair spread about her and showing an endearing and previously unnoticed tendency to curl, made him feel she let him in on a wonderful secret.

"Come here." He piled the pillows behind her and helped her sit up.

When he began to wipe away the sticky mess, she caught his wrist. "Thank you."

"It's the least a gentleman can do."

"That's not what I mean."

He met her gaze. She looked tired and replete. "So now you know there's nothing wrong with you?"

It still boggled the mind that Crewe hadn't been able to satisfy his wife. She was desire incarnate.

"You know, some people say I have a sharp tongue, and a few brave souls accuse me of intellectual arrogance."

He wrung out the cloth and stroked between her legs. Her lack of self-consciousness was unexpected and gratifying. "Brave to the point of foolhardy." His amusement faded. "You're the kind of woman a man longs for all his life. Passionate. Responsive. Generous. Beautiful."

"West, you wax poetic."

The sardonic response didn't rattle him. The change from sweetness to irony meant she was afraid. Right now, his Helena scrambled to restore damaged defenses.

He'd let her do that. Because no defense could keep him out, not when he'd been deep inside her and touched her soul.

"Don't I just?" He set the bowl on the floor and slid into bed beside her. "Move over."

"Are you staying?"

"You said you wanted to talk. And as always, I'm your humble servant."

"Not so humble."

How true. They were both proud creatures. If they weren't, they'd have found their way back to each other before this. "No, not so humble. Shall I stay?"

"Yes, please." With beguiling eagerness, she curled up beside him.

He pulled the covers up. Now he wasn't mad to possess this woman within the next minute, the air was cold on his bare skin. Helena had whipped him into a frenzy where nothing else mattered. He could hardly wait for her to do it again.

When she leaned her head on his shoulder, his embrace firmed. Generally he didn't linger to cuddle and confide. But his gut knotted in denial at the thought of leaving this bed. "Comfortable?"

"Oh, yes." She tipped her face up. "By the way, I was thanking you for something else entirely."

He smiled. "Gad, what an obliging fellow I must be, if you have so much to thank me for."

She arched her eyebrows, but didn't squash his pretensions. "If you want to corner me into marrying you, a pregnancy is a powerful bargaining chip."

West shrugged. "I don't need to cheat to win."

She tensed without moving away. "So you're still committed to that nonsensical proposal?"

After what they'd just done, nonsensical was the last thing he'd call making Helena his wife. "We settled on an affair."

"While we're here."

"Until you choose to end it." He dipped his head to kiss her shoulder. She smelled delectable. Warm, sated woman. "Let's not quarrel."

Surprisingly, she didn't disagree. If what they'd done had changed him—and he was still discovering how much—it seemed to have changed her, too.

She relaxed and rubbed her cheek against his shoulder. The artless, affectionate gesture set his heart stuttering in a way that should worry him. But he was too damned pleased with life to seek out trouble.

"Precautions were unnecessary."

Some women tracked the weeks to work out the safest times for a tumble. Given Helena hadn't taken a lover since Crewe, he hadn't expected her to bother. "I've never trusted the counting method."

She shook her head. "Nothing so complicated. My best guess is I'm barren. There was never any sign that I'd conceived with Crewe."

"You forbade him your bed."

"After a year or so. He was attentive at the beginning—however many other women he pursued at the same time."

"I'd kill him for you if I could."

Her gaze was puzzled. "You sound like you mean that."

"Believe me, lovely, I do."

She stretched up to kiss him. A contact without heat, steeped in friendship. Odd that it should shake him as deeply as those voracious kisses when he'd been inside her.

"Thank you." With a sigh, she settled back against him. "I'm sorry I spent all these years blaming you. It was childish. My disastrous marriage is my fault."

West sat up abruptly, dislodging her from his chest. "You were a naïve girl, just seventeen, and Crewe set out to snare you."

She looked troubled, lying upon the pillows and staring up at him from fathomless black eyes. "I should have been clever enough to see what he was."

"At that stage, few people did. In his younger days, he did his best to hide his vices. I'd known him longer than you, and I assumed like most of us, he sowed a few wild oats before settling down. And he could be damned charming when he wanted something. You didn't stand a chance. You've stopped blaming me for what happened. It's time to stop blaming yourself."

He watched her consider his statement without accepting it. By God, before they left Woodley, he'd convince her to forgive herself, or die trying. "I have a suspicion about Crewe."

Her lips twitched. "I had lots of suspicions about Crewe. Most of which unfortunately proved true."

"For a man who scattered his seed far and wide, I never heard he fathered a bastard."

"Oh? Perhaps he was careful."

Not bloody likely. "Perhaps he was sterile."

A faint line appeared between her marked black brows. "The opium and brandy can't have helped."

West shrugged and lay down, sliding his arm around her. "It's purely a theory. But if you're embarking on a life of sin, don't rely too much on past history."

"A life of sin?"

He smiled at her. "Obviously I'd like you to sin with me alone."

Her lips flattened in disapproval. "That would be like getting married."

"Perish the thought."

A surprisingly peaceful silence fell as she snuggled against him. What a night it had been—and a million miles from what he'd expected. He hadn't been sure he'd manage to steal a kiss, and now they were lovers.

"Are you tired?" she murmured after a long while. She inched one hand under the sheet and across his belly.

West, who had lapsed into a pleasant reverie, went on instant alert. "Are you?"

Her black eyes sparked with devilry. She looked like the spirited girl, not the self-contained and acerbic widow he'd known in London. "We're only here another week. Time's a-wasting."

With one powerful movement, he rolled over her, staring down into a face alight with laughter and desire. "I've acquired an imperious mistress."

Her hands ran up his chest and linked behind his neck. "Aren't you lucky?"

"Aren't I just?" His cock hardened and nudged between her legs. One part of him wasn't sleepy at all.

She kissed him, her mouth hot and eager. While his tongue swept between her lips, he toyed with her nipple. She tilted her hips in brazen invitation.

Sizzling sensual pleasure beckoned. West wasn't a man to say no.

CHAPTER EIGHT

When Helena wandered downstairs the next day, it was close to noon. She made her way to the morning room where Caro and Fenella sat gossiping over tea.

West's theory that her fellow Dashing Widows were too spellbound to notice much else around them was borne out. Helena was a notorious early riser—most days in London she rode in Hyde Park at dawn—but neither of her friends questioned her tardy appearance.

Helena fell upon the tea table with enthusiasm. A night of debauchery played havoc with a polite appetite.

"That's a pretty dress," Fenella said from the couch near the fire. As usual, she had her embroidery on her lap. "I haven't seen it before."

With a self-conscious gesture, Helena's hand strayed to the high lace neckline. She'd bought the yellow and white gown last season, but had decided she didn't like its Elizabethan collar. She had no idea why her maid had packed it. But when she'd looked in her mirror this morning and seen the marks of West's teeth, she'd decided this dress was her latest favorite. "It's new."

"More demure than you usually wear," Caro said from the sofa.

Helena's cheeks heated. Making a great show of filling her cup, she avoided her friends' eyes. "I feel like a change of style. Would either of you like tea?"

"I'll ring for more," Caro said. "That's been sitting there for half an hour."

While Caro summoned a footman and arranged more refreshments, Helena sought a seat in the room's darkest corner. Luckily it was a typical February day, gray, wet, miserable. Gloomy. Despite copious amounts of Milk of Roses, her face was still pink with whisker burn. Tonight, she'd make sure that West shaved before he came to her, however exciting his beard had felt rasping against her skin.

Tonight...

How odd it felt to anticipate a meeting with a lover. And what a lover. She shivered to recall the way his mouth had explored every inch of her. From her toes to her eyebrows and everything—everything!—in between. She shifted on her brocade chair and stifled a gasp of discomfort. Today her body ached in so many unfamiliar places.

"Amy's back the day after tomorrow," Caro said, returning to her place without glancing at Helena, which was a good thing. She feared she looked completely besotted.

The woeful fact was that she felt completely besotted. She put it down to discovering sexual fulfillment so late in life. But right now, her logical world was awash with butterflies and unicorns and rainbows.

"I've never met her," Fen said. "She lives here most of the time, doesn't she?"

"Yes," Helena said. "She does a jolly good job of running the place. She might be only seventeen, but she's quite the expert on modern farming. The rest of the family arrives the day before the wedding."

Heaven help her, she'd better get a grip on her reactions before her sister turned up. Amy had the sharpest eyes in England—and the least discretion. It was lucky she was staying with one of their aunts right now, or Helena's fall from grace would no longer be a secret.

"It's a pity Robert couldn't be here, too," Caro said. "He's mapping some obscure corner of the African coast and couldn't get leave."

"I haven't met him either," Fen said.

"He stayed with Helena last year in London, when he'd just come back from New South Wales. He's frightfully handsome and gallant and naval."

"Oh, I'm sure he sets hearts fluttering."

Helena smiled. "Ladies are swooning between here and Sydney, and every port in between."

"I hope this weather doesn't worsen before the wedding," Fen said as the butler brought in a laden tray. "Travel's so difficult if there's heavy snow."

"All the Nashes are punishing riders," Caro said, as Fen rose to serve the tea. "Silas's relations would push through a blizzard to be here."

As Helena sipped a fresh cup of tea, she'd gathered enough composure to ask after West without sounding like a complete nitwit. "Where are the gentlemen?"

"Silas's horse was favoring its right foreleg this morning," Caro said, setting her cup into its saucer. "They're in the stables seeing to the problem."

"Silas and West are. Anthony's just gone along for show," Fen said serenely, wandering back to her couch with a full cup. "The poor darling doesn't know one end of a horse from another."

"But he could out-sail the other two with his hands tied behind his back," Helena said. In recent weeks, she'd become very fond of Anthony Townsend. She admired both his acumen and his lack of artifice. And his devotion to Fenella, who had emerged from long grief to find happiness with him.

"I'm sure a prime whip like Fen appreciates a man who lets her take the reins," Caro said. "If she married an arrogant brute like West, he'd never let her drive."

"He's not an arrogant brute," Helena said, then dipped her head in mortification.

A resonant silence fell.

"You've changed your tune." Caro cast her a

quizzical glance. "He's always set your back up. I've never been sure why. I think he's utterly divine."

So divine that before she fell in love with Silas, Caro had considered taking West as a lover. With an audible clink, Helena returned her cup to its saucer. She knew she was absurd—Caro was mad about Silas—but the idea of West kissing her friend made Helena want to shoot her.

Telling herself to settle down, she affected an airy tone. "He's back from Russia with some of the stuffing knocked out of him. As a result, he's more bearable than usual."

Bravo. That was much more like her.

"I'm worried about this fever," Fen said, sipping her tea with a thoughtful frown. "Anthony says he's seen agues like this in the East, and they can recur for years."

"This sounds a very odd diplomatic mission," Caro said. "Away for months, and traipsing all over Russia."

"Anthony says Russia's a strange place," Fen said.

"And of course if Anthony says it, it must be true," Helena said slyly.

When Fen blushed, she looked like a pretty sixteen-year-old. "I'm sorry. I must sound addled. Love turns the brain to custard."

Lust had a similar effect, Helena could now confirm.

"So true," Caro said. "The other day, I was walking in the woods, and I started thinking about Silas. I got completely lost."

The reminiscent light in Caro's eyes hinted there was more to the story. Since they'd found love, Helena had noted the changes in her friends. But today she was hypersensitive to the female satisfaction pervading the room.

"It's a large estate," Helena said.

"I got as far as the Grecian temple before Silas found me."

Ideal for a private rendezvous. When she'd been a giddy girl, Helena and West had often met there.

"We're hardly Dashing Widows anymore," Fenella said with a smile. "Perhaps we should rechristen ourselves the dreamy ladies."

Helena expected someone to mention the one unattached Dashing Widow, but Caro started to describe her forthcoming voyage to China instead. Helen let the chatter wash over her, while she wallowed in wanton memories.

Last night, West had answered so many of her questions.

Was she unnatural? Not with the right lover.

What fueled the light in her friends' eyes? She now had a fair idea.

Tonight West would come to her bed again. And perhaps this time, he wouldn't leave her unsettled, as well as supremely satisfied.

Because every answer she'd received had raised a hundred questions. And all of them disturbed her. How could a physical act conjure such a profound emotional effect? She knew it was mere imagination, but when West thrust deep inside her, she'd felt like they united into a single being.

"Helena?"

She emerged from her reverie to find both Caro and Fen staring at her.

"Sorry. I wandered off." She struggled to sound like her sharp-tongued self, not this moony creature she'd become. "You can't blame me. I've heard nothing but China and weddings—and wedding china!—since I arrived."

Caro smiled. "It must be dull for you, with Fen and I so preoccupied."

Did the question hide a sting? After all, she was still on the shelf—at least as far as her friends knew. How shocked they'd be to learn what she'd done last night. Shocked, and quick to interfere.

But Caro's smile was genuine. "This is our last chance to be together for a long while."

Helena picked up her tea and said with perfect sincerity, "I'm delighted you're both so happy—and I heartily approve of your choices. Silas is the best brother in the world. I look forward to you becoming my sister in fact as well as in my heart, Caro. And, Fen, I'd never pictured you with a man like Anthony, but you're perfect for each other."

Caro's regard was mocking. "Oh, dear, I'm not picking up a single note of irony. Are you sickening for something, Hel? Perhaps you should go upstairs and lie down."

Only if West comes, too, she wanted to say.

She gave a short laugh. "It's the blasted atmosphere in this house. Even I can't help getting mawkish. I promise everything will return to normal, once we've packed away the wedding finery."

Fen studied her. "Helena, things will change, that's inevitable, but our friendship will endure. I hope you'll be a regular visitor to the Beeches."

"Thank you. I plan to come down and inspect the stables the minute you're back from your wedding trip." The Townsends were setting up home with Fenella's son and Anthony's ward at a magnificent estate outside Winchester.

Fenella stepped straight into the heart of a family. Helena suffered a pang of envy, before forcibly reminding herself that she preferred the freedom to make her own choices.

Caro looked out the window. "Speaking of stables, our menfolk are marching across the lawn in this direction."

Helena had last seen West when he'd reluctantly crawled out of her bed before dawn. Now at his approach, her silly heart leaped about with excitement like a dog before a walk.

With a brilliant smile, Caro rose to open the door onto the terrace. "Come inside, out of the cold."

As he stepped in, Silas gave her a brief kiss. Anthony crossed to sit beside Fenella and sling one powerful arm around her. West entered more slowly, closing the door behind him. His eyes arrowed in on Helena, before he made a great show of turning to Caro. "The horse just needs rest, in my opinion."

Helena slid her cup and saucer onto the table so that their rattle didn't betray her reaction to West's arrival. She hadn't felt like this since she was a young girl, infatuated with her handsome neighbor.

Her neighbor was still handsome. Seeing him, her heart slammed to a stop, then began to beat hard and fast.

Luckily nobody paid her a shred of attention. She had a horrible feeling that if they did, they'd know precisely what she and West had been up to all night.

Silas was talking about his lame horse, but he may as well have been speaking Greek. Although if he'd spoken Greek, Helena might have made an effort to concentrate—like all the Nash offspring, she'd had a good classical education. But her friends' voices turned into mere background as her eyes devoured West, leaning with louche elegance against the doorframe.

She knew exactly how that tall, rangy form looked unclothed. Those long, capable fingers had been inside her body. That ruthless mouth had tasted her sex and licked her into writhing ecstasy.

Heat flared in the pit of her stomach. She wanted him now. Right this minute.

His shoulders tensed, as if he knew what she was

thinking. After one smoldering glance, he concentrated with unconvincing interest on Silas.

Helena curled her fingernails into her palms until the sting forced her back to reality. What she and West had unleashed last night threatened to break free of all constraint.

CHAPTER NINE

*a*gain West left Helena before dawn. The urge to cling to him, and let scandal go hang nearly overpowered what little remained of her good sense. The bed felt very lonely and cold once he'd gone.

She slept late and awoke to a sweet smell. Her eyes opened to see a pink lily on her pillow—the exotic perfume combined with West's lingering, musky scent.

Gently she touched the petals, her mind full of the night's pleasures. After he left her, West must have raided Silas's extravagant greenhouses. As befitted one of the nation's premier botanists, Silas had massive heated conservatories attached to the house. Convenient when one planned a wedding in February.

Helena held the lily to her nose and rolled over to find a sealed note propped on her nightstand. After the flood of correspondence from Russia, she recognized the slashing writing.

She pushed herself up on the pillows and reached for the letter. Idly she turned it over and over in her hands, until she realized she was smiling down at it like a sapskull. As if this was a love note.

Damn this house. The atmosphere of romance triumphant was irresistible.

Still, her heart skipped as she slid her thumbnail under the seal and unfolded the thick creamy sheet of paper.

My darling...

Blindly she glanced away. The endearment shouldn't be so powerful. After those letters from Russia, she'd decided West used words like sweetheart and darling without meaning anything much by them.

Neither of them pretended that this affair involved love. Pleasure certainly. And she was grateful that they'd moved beyond past bitterness to re-establish their friendship. She'd forgotten how she enjoyed his humor, and the way he wouldn't back down from her.

If he was here, she'd scold him for putting a romantic gloss on an unromantic union. But still when he called her his darling, her blood turned to syrup. She hoped to heaven she wasn't going to end up going silly over West.

That would be the last straw.

The first two words of his note had her in such a spin that she'd failed to read the rest. Skating her eyes across "darling," she went on.

Meet me at the Greek temple at 12. Don't worry about

*the others. They think I've invited you to Shelton Abbey to
see my stables.*

Yours in sensual anticipation.
West

Helena rode Artemis through the bare woods, toward
the isolated summerhouse her father had built after his
marriage. A happy marriage that had endured until her
parents' death in a carriage accident near Pompeii
three years ago. The Nashes made a habit of happy
marriages. Helena couldn't doubt how well Caro and
Silas suited each other.

Her disastrous union with Crewe had been the
exception to the rule.

After two nights in West's arms, the memory of her
pig of a husband didn't bring the usual churning stomach. Right now, life was too interesting for her to dwell
on old failures.

The forest was breathlessly still as Helena
approached the pretty little folly. The only sound was
the crunch of Artemis's neat hooves on the leaf litter.
Above them, a watery sun shone in a streaky sky. The
late winter day carried the promise of spring.

Or perhaps, despite her best efforts to keep a cool
head, Helena wasn't immune to the thrill of sneaking
away to meet a handsome lover.

Through the trees, the lake glistened. With sudden vigor, she set her heels to Artemis's sides. The mare broke into a springing canter.

Helena supposed now West was back in England, she'd have to return the horse. Which would break her heart. Unless she could budge him on selling Artemis. And long acquaintance told her that when he made up his mind, nothing shifted him.

West stood on the graceful flight of marble steps, watching her ride up. She shivered at his intense concentration on her. Once she'd found it unnerving. Not now when she knew where that interest led.

Predatory intent filled his smile. "I wish I could paint."

Helena drew Artemis to a halt. "Oh, no, not today, my fine fellow. I have other plans for you. And none of them involve standing several feet away with a brush in your hand."

He ran lightly down the steps. He looked well, more like the man she remembered, before he fell victim to that mysterious fever. "Lady Crewe, you put me to the blush."

"Blush, fine. Brush, no," she said with a laugh, as he lifted her from the sidesaddle to the dry winter grass.

West caught her up for an urgent kiss, then drew back and cradled her head in his hands, holding her still for a thorough inspection.

She shifted restlessly under his searching gaze, not just because that kiss had stirred her blood. "What?"

"How is it that I've only been away from you for a couple of hours, yet I've missed you like the very devil?"

"Don't be absurd," she said, struggling for an acerbic tone, but instead sounding bewildered and enchanted.

"I want to go where we can be alone for day after glorious day. Where I can wake to sunlight and make uninhibited love to you. Where when I get the urge in a drawing room, I can bend you over the back of the couch. Where we can talk until late in front of the fire. I want you to myself. I don't want to have to check the clock or look over my shoulder for fear of scandal."

His voice was insistent, strong emotion deepening it to a growly bass that made her bones vibrate. She struggled to escape this net of attraction, that tangled tighter with every second. But it was so damned difficult, when she, too, already kicked against the restrictions of secrecy.

"You speak as if our liaison will outlast this week."

Mockery lit his eyes. "You still mean to toss me out of your bed in a few days? I don't believe it."

The problem was that she wasn't sure she believed it either.

"That was the arrangement." Curse her for sounding so uncertain.

"A week isn't enough."

She jerked free, bumping into Artemis who snorted and sidled away. "What are you suggesting?"

"You know what I'm suggesting."

Unfortunately she did. "I don't want to marry again."

"Then let's be lovers."

She shook her head. "We can't keep sneaking around. And such things always become public knowledge."

He frowned, more in puzzlement than anger. "Would that be so bad? You're not a debutante, and you were faithful to Crewe when he didn't deserve it. Society will cast a forgiving eye on a discreet affair."

"I don't want people talking about me. I had enough of that when I was married. Everyone gossiped about Crewe, and by default, me. I hated how they watched me all the time. I hated their pity and contempt."

He didn't bother contradicting her. They both knew she was right. Playing the part of the wronged wife had lacerated her pride to tatters. "Then come away with me. We can go to France or Italy. Or darkest Africa, for all that. I don't care as long as we're together."

Wonderingly she stared at him. "West, you almost sound desperate."

He gave a self-derisive grunt of laughter and dropped to sit on the steps leading to the Doric-columned doorway. "How the mighty have fallen." He ran his hand through his hair, and his expression was rueful. "I'm sorry. I meant today to be an idyll, yet here I am haranguing you."

For a moment, she studied him. He was by nature

the king of the beasts, but she found these occasional hints of vulnerability so dangerously appealing.

Abruptly she turned away, as if she stared too long at the sun. She caught Artemis and took off her bridle, so the mare was free to graze on the sparse greenery. The Arab was too well trained to bolt. Even if she did, they were within walking distance of the house, however secluded this pretty haven seemed.

Only when she'd gained a grip on her rioting emotions did Helena face West again. He lounged in front of her. She'd always been conscious of his handsomeness, although as an adult, she'd had little difficulty resisting his practiced charms. But here where they'd roamed as children, it was impossible to keep her distance. Without his shell of worldly sophistication, he seemed much more real. And much more perilous to her vow never to fall victim to another libertine.

Except right now, he didn't look like a libertine. He looked like a man who could be well satisfied with the right woman. Even his clothes seemed honest. Shirtsleeves, fawn breeches, and scuffed boots that had seen better days.

Fearing that the battle to keep her distance was all but lost, she sighed. She sat beside him, taking his hand. "West, let's enjoy our day. After tomorrow, we'll have to be more careful. Amy's back, and when it comes to secrets, she's got a nose like a foxhound."

"You know, we don't need to hide our attachment at

Woodley Park. It's not as if the others are sleeping in chaste isolation." He turned his hand to lace his fingers through hers.

Fear rippled through her anew. She could countenance incendiary passion. After all, that was why she'd entered into this affair. But these affectionate gestures reached deep into her soul—and her soul wasn't up for negotiation.

"Yes, we do," she said, withdrawing her hand. "If the others think you and I are interested in each other, they'll nag us into the ground until we marry."

"They already know I'm interested in you."

"They don't know I'm interested back," she retorted, wondering if she betrayed too much. Although he must know she was helpless against his lures. "And if there's even a hint of a scandal, the wedding guests will carry it back to London."

"I don't mind."

"I do." And wondered why her words rang hollow.

He rose and extended his hand. "If you're going to argue with me, come inside. I'm not dressed for outdoors."

She accepted his hand, and the tacit request for a change of subject. "Surely you can't be cold. Not after Russia. I remember in one of your letters, you said that the air was so freezing, it hurt to breathe."

He gave a grunt of pleased surprise. "So you did read my letters?"

She shot him a teasing look. "One or two."

"More than that, I suspect."

She laughed. "All right. I'll admit it."

"So they didn't end up fueling the drawing room fire?"

"No, of course not. They're marvelous letters. I've read and re-read them. There's one about racing troikas at dawn across the frozen steppes that I know by heart. I could almost hear the snow crunching under the runners, and the bells tinkling on the horses' harness. For a careless libertine, you have quite a way with words."

It had been a game, pretending to despise that copious, fascinating correspondence. But in the last two days, the game between them had changed forever, and she could never claim indifference again. Not that her indifference had ever convinced him. "There. Look as smug as you like."

He did look smug. "I always knew you read them. After all, you occasionally replied."

"I couldn't let you get away with talking about breeding rights, could I?"

"For Artemis."

She shot him a skeptical look. "If you say so."

He put on a theatrically innocent look. "I was lonely in Russia. You can't blame me for pondering…natural matters."

A huff of ironic laughter. "I've reached the conclusion that you think about natural matters most of the time."

He caught her close for a quick kiss, an explicit promise of more to come. "A man needs a hobby."

Helena caught his hand, and they ascended the stairs together. "Do you remember we used to come here that summer before you went to Oxford?"

"I do. Those are among my most precious memories."

She frowned as they stepped through the tall door. "I'm sure that's not true. We were very innocent."

"That was part of the charm." He smiled with that singular sweetness that she found increasingly difficult to withstand. A sweetness he seemed to direct at her alone.

She tore her gaze from his face, if only to hide how close she came to giving him everything he asked. And released a gasp of delight. "West, this is magical."

The marble summerhouse wasn't designed for February days, even fine ones like today. But he'd set braziers around a circular table covered in cream silk. Savory scents rose from porcelain dishes, and a bottle of champagne sat in an ice bucket.

West helped her remove her vermillion riding jacket. Another light kiss, before he stepped away to lift the champagne bottle. "I'm glad you approve."

Helena shifted closer to the table, battling the urge to cry, silly as it was. "You took such pains."

His eyes were disconcertingly perceptive. "I ordered a few servants around. They were glad of the occupation. With Silas and Caro so wrapped up in each other, they're at a loose end."

"No, you devoted real thought to this." Her voice was husky.

"Perhaps a moment or two. And don't worry—I told the staff I wanted to give you a treat before I took you over to my stables. I made everything sound aboveboard."

Pleasure and surprise vanquished reticence. "It's the nicest thing anyone's ever done for me."

His smile was tender. "That's a crime. A woman like you should have swains scattering roses in front of her wherever she goes."

She gave a cracked laugh. "That doesn't sound very practical." She took in the massed flowers adorning the table and set in vases around the room. "Anyway, I prefer lilies."

The champagne cork popped, and he filled two crystal glasses. "You always did."

He'd remembered her favorite flower? She'd thought this morning's lily was just a happy accident. God in heaven, she was in dire trouble. If he hadn't gone to such effort—and if she wasn't completely under his spell—she'd take to her heels.

She swallowed and tried to sound relaxed and amused. But the hand she curled around her glass trembled. "I hope you left a few flowers. There's a wedding next week."

West raised his glass to her, and while his tone was

cheerful, something momentous swam in his eyes. "One or two. Caro will have her bouquet."

"No lilies, though." The champagne was cold and crisp on her tongue, and did nothing to combat her giddiness.

He pulled out a chair for her. "There's plenty of other flowers."

Helena sat, unfolded her damask napkin, and placed it across her lap. "One of the benefits of marrying a botanist is that Caro will never lack for floral tributes."

West dropped a kiss on her shoulder, making her shiver with anticipation. So far, his caresses had remained circumspect, but impending pleasure hummed around them. This meeting in the temple would have a very different end from those clandestine encounters when she was sixteen.

"Nor should you." He sat and caught the hand she'd laid on the table, bringing it to his lips. "Be happy, sweet Helena. Everything will work out one way or another."

CHAPTER TEN

*W*est leaned back from the table and raised a glass of excellent claret to his lips as he studied Helena. Right now, she didn't look like the self-contained countess with the formidable brain, who had alternately awed and fascinated London society. Nor did she, thank God, look like the unhappy Lady Crewe who had held her head high through the shambles her repugnant husband had made of her life.

She didn't even look like the adorably unsure beauty who had succumbed to his seduction.

Was that only two nights ago? He'd lived a lifetime since.

He smiled at her in delight. "My dear Lady Crewe, you're foxed."

Helena smiled back with bleary affability. "I fear, my lord, you are right."

With impressive steadiness, she raised her claret and took a sip. Between them, the ruins of their meal spread across the table. Silas's kitchens had done them proud, with oysters, chicken *à la perse,* salads—courtesy again of the greenhouses—exotic fruits, fresh and candied. All that remained in one piece was a meringue fancy molded in the shape of the summerhouse.

West wasn't anywhere near tipsy, although an enjoyable warmth simmered in his blood. He had a strong head for liquor. The only man able to drink him under the table was Anthony Townsend, who had clearly led quite a life, running his shipping line.

The only man in England. In Russia, the locals and their vodka had trumped him.

Helena, on the other hand, was three sheets to the wind.

"Do you want to lie down?" He waved his glass toward the low divan under the window, where the servants had set out cushions and rugs.

Salacious anticipation broadened her smile. "Yes."

When her foot curled over his knee in unmistakable invitation, he jumped like a virgin. During the meal, she must have kicked off her half-boots.

His cock reacted with predictable enthusiasm. Never had he been as desperate for a woman as he was for Helena. She merely had to look at him sideways, and he was upright as a ship's mast. He'd long believed they'd prove a physical match, but the sizzling reality of holding her in his arms surpassed all his imaginings.

Still, a gentleman didn't take advantage of a lady's inebriation.

And he remained a gentleman. Just.

"You'll feel better after a nap."

She pursed her lips and lowered her eyelids until thick, black lashes shadowed her cheekbones. "I'm feeling rather fine right now."

With unmistakable intent, her foot slid further up his thigh. His grip on the glass tightened as explosions set off behind his eyes. "Helena, you're in no state to make decisions."

He wished she'd stop smiling at him as though she meant to gobble him up for dessert, instead of the sugar and cream confection.

"That charming bower screams sin. You can't mean to waste it."

"We'll use it when you've got a clear head."

With a soft laugh, she curled her toes against his leg. "I'm never clearheaded when I'm with you."

Astonishment, as much as burgeoning arousal, had him sitting straight in his chair. From Helena, that was a major admission. Unfortunately, it also proved that she wasn't herself.

He caught that brazen stockinged foot before it ventured higher. "We've got all afternoon. Silas and Caro are visiting the neighbors, and Fen and Anthony are looking at property in the area."

"Then let's not waste time."

"I can't seduce a woman who's drunk," he said tartly.

Despite his tone, he couldn't help caressing the long, elegant foot in his lap. He loved that she was built like a greyhound, all slim speed and grace.

In response to his touch, her lids lowered further. "Very well."

Curiosity stilled his stroking hand. "Very well?"

"Yes." A beat of silence. "Because I intend to seduce you."

West's heart crashed into his ribs, and the world went black. That low, husky voice should have a danger sign posted on it. He blinked to bring her back into focus. "Hel…"

With taunting languor, she untied the masculine cravat around her neck and dropped it to the tiled floor. Her index finger strayed down her throat to pause at the high collar of her white shirt. All the moisture dried from West's mouth, as his gaze fastened on that teasing hand.

"I'm not drunk, West," she murmured. "Just nicely merry."

"Nonetheless…" The word emerged as a croak, while he watched her flick the top pearl button open to reveal a few inches of creamy skin. Every muscle tightened in expectation. Which was ridiculous when that very morning, he'd seen her stark naked.

But there was something so damned stirring about a woman proclaiming her desire in the middle of the day. At any time of the day, really.

Helena was the most imaginative person he knew.

The prospect of her devoting all that creativity to his pleasure made him shake.

Another button. Another few inches of skin.

West licked parched lips, and assured himself that she knew what she was doing.

He had to touch her, or go mad. His hand reached up under her skirts to release her garter and slide the silk stocking down. The brush of his fingers on her bare instep made her gasp, but her tone stayed cool. "You've taught me a lot about persuasion. It's time I put those lessons into practice."

Two more buttons. The shirt parted to reveal a narrow line of smooth olive skin.

She toyed with a third. His hungry eyes fastened on the finger moving over the button in a fiendishly suggestive pattern.

And something struck him that should have struck him much earlier.

"You're not wearing a corset," he said in a strangled voice.

A faint smile lifted her lush lips. "Or a shift."

He closed his eyes, but the image of Helena undressing little by little for his delectation remained burned on his vision. "God give me strength."

"I'm not wearing drawers either."

His eyes shot open. He should be used to the way she sent his heart hurtling around his chest. He wasn't. "That's why you rode sidesaddle."

Those lips quirked. "Yes."

Caught up in the pleasure of having her to himself, he hadn't paid too much attention to how she'd arrived. In London, she followed the dictates of propriety, however reluctantly. Here at Woodley Park, she almost always rode astride.

"You'll drive me out of my mind before you've finished," he groaned, his hand clenching on her toes.

"That's the general idea."

To his regret, she lowered her foot. With dazed eyes, he watched her stand and step away from the table with a sway of the hips and a saucy backward glance. Now that he knew how few layers separated her skin from his greedy hands, his restraint frayed until it was threadbare.

With a theatrical slowness that threatened to send him up in flames, she shifted to the side, raised her foot to the chair, and hitched up her skirts. By the time she'd untied her second garter and rolled the stocking off, he vibrated with lust.

When she straightened and faced him, his attention fixed on her open shirt. Every movement offered shadowy glimpses of her breasts. Tantalizing because she remained covered. Mostly.

He licked his lips when her nipples hardened against the white cambric.

She sent him a direct look. "This morning when I dressed, I was perfectly sober. So your scruples, while admirable, are unnecessary."

He was on his feet before he thought about it and

stalking toward her. She raised her hand to his chest, stopping him.

"No."

"What the devil?" His hands opened and closed at his sides. She'd played this tormenting game the first night. He wasn't sure he'd survive another bout.

Her glittering gaze focused on his face. "I want to test my wiles."

He closed his eyes, and his groan was pained. A different game, after all. But the same torture. "This is revenge for that time I pushed you in the horse trough, isn't it?"

"Would I hold a grudge for something a young lout did twenty years ago?"

He opened wary eyes. "Absolutely."

"You know me so well. Now take off your shirt."

With shaking hands, he dragged the shirt over his head and dropped it to the tiled floor. He felt like he possessed ten thumbs, and not particularly deft ones at that. Thank God, he wasn't wearing a neck cloth. The braziers warmed the air, but the sensual purpose in Helena's eyes set him shivering in anticipation.

"Are you cold?" She moved around him like an art connoisseur admiring a statue. Except this connoisseur had bare feet and looked likely to fall out of her shirt any moment.

"Anything but."

On the tiles, her feet were soundless. But he knew to the second when she padded close behind him, even before her breath warmed his nape. Every nerve went on alert, but she didn't touch him. Instead he heard her inhale deeply.

"Why do you always smell so good? I believe I could live on the air around you."

"Hel…" he bit out. "Stop teasing me."

"I've only started," she whispered in his ear and nipped his earlobe.

Need juddered through him. "For pity's sake."

"No pity." She trailed one finger along his bare shoulder, and his cock swelled in immediate answer. "Sit down, and I'll help with your boots."

Giddy with rising desire, he let her lead him to the platform in the alcove. She pulled him round to face her, then pushed. When he collapsed among the pillows, she stood tall over him, a commanding, gorgeous mistress well worth the winning.

He adored her lack of shyness. Still, he wasn't quite ready to surrender his accustomed mastery. "You know, it would be dashed easy for you to sit on me."

Her laugh was sheer temptation. "Why the rush?"

His hips bumped up, his rod straining against the front of his breeches. "I'm a simple creature. Show me a brandy, and I want to drink it. Show me a chunk of roast beef, and I want to eat it. Show me a comely woman, and I want to—"

"I can imagine," she hurried to say, before he reached the profane ending. "But you're not getting your way."

"Helena," he growled in dismay, flopping back.

"Yet."

Yet...

West could live with "yet." He smiled up at the ceiling where simpering amoretti circled a complacent Zeus. Above the window, a large swan eyed a fat blonde's abundant charms with lascivious intent. Once such a woman might have roused his interest. These days, his taste was for domineering brunettes.

He couldn't help thinking he had the advantage over the king of the gods. Even if his mistress meant to test him before welcoming him to paradise.

His attention turned to Helena as she dropped to her knees. The skirt preserved her modesty, but did nothing to rein in his unruly imagination. Fresh desire jolted him.

With characteristic competence, she tugged at his boots. Seeing her kneeling sparked inevitable fantasies of her mouth on his cock. As she moved to his other boot, he speculated on how long he'd need before he banished her inhibitions. Today's startling role reversal hinted that she might enjoy a daring variation or two.

Including that one.

He'd drifted off so thoroughly into a dream of Helena pleasuring him that her voice came as a shock. "Don't go to sleep."

His gaze fixed on Leda's plump nakedness. Yes, he was definitely ahead of Zeus. At least today. "I've had two interrupted nights, you know."

"You didn't seem to mind at the time." Those adept hands ripped at the buttons on his breeches. No shyness indeed. Praise every angel in heaven. "Lift your hips."

He obeyed with alacrity. One long tug, and he lay naked before her, back resting on the divan, legs spread across the tiles on either side of her, cock hard against his belly.

"I like your body very much," she murmured. With a few quick movements, she released her hair. That moment when it unfurled from contained elegance to lavish profusion always stole his breath. "Although someone needs to feed you up."

West didn't want to think about his illness. He didn't want to think at all. "The only thing I want to eat right now is you."

With a sinuous grace that had his heart performing a Highland reel, she slithered up his body. The glancing contact set off fireworks in his head until he couldn't see anything else but her. If she meant to torture him all afternoon, he wasn't sure he'd survive the experience.

"Later," she said, but the rough note in her voice told him that she liked the idea.

He loved licking her to climax. Damn it, he loved every single thing they did together. If she stuck to her word and sent him away after her brother's wedding, he'd be in a bad way indeed. When Silas had been sick with longing for Caro, West recalled feeling faintly superior. This time round, he had a horrible feeling the joke might be on him.

Helena rose over him, shirt gaping to reveal her perfect breasts at last. Unable to resist, he reached to cup them.

Jerking up, she straddled him.

"No." She caught his wrists and pulled him away.

"I need to touch you."

"First I'm going to touch you."

"We can touch each other." Air seemed in short supply.

"If we do, you'll take over."

"Don't you like me to take over?"

"Don't be a clod, West. Of course I do." Her impatient affection pierced his heart. "I'm conducting an experiment, and I don't want any interruptions."

He laughed. "You and your experiments. Heaven help the man involved with a scholarly woman."

"I'm not feeling too sorry for you." She leaned down, still holding his hands, and kissed him thoroughly, using her tongue to stoke his craving.

Who needed air? He drowned in swirling heat. Her silky hair fell about them like a shining ebony curtain. By the time she raised her head, he was panting.

"I mean to be bold," she said in the same tone young Helena had used when she'd boasted that she'd ride the wildest horse in her father's stables. And by God, she'd done it, too.

"I hope so," he said hoarsely.

Before he had a chance to calm his blood's maniac rush, she stood and undid the last button. She freed the shirt from her waistband and shrugged it away.

For a moment, she stood proudly before him, bare-breasted and splendid. With her extravagant mane of black hair, she looked like some primitive deity.

Leda, you're not even in the race.

Every time he saw Helena like this, it felt like a gift. His hands curled into the satin cushions piled beneath him. "You're a beautiful creature."

"For a woman plotting lechery, you're a fine sight yourself." She tugged at the tapes on her skirt and let it fall to the floor.

West sighed with masculine appreciation as she sauntered naked toward him. Dear God, she was magnificent.

She came down over him on all fours. He groaned and lurched up to press closer.

That autocratic hand pushed him down. "Not yet."

"That answer is rapidly losing its charm."

"I still like it." She dipped her head and nibbled an incendiary path down his neck to his shoulder, where she bit him. He grunted at the sting, but let her have her way. Then her hands and mouth seemed to be everywhere. His arms, his chest, his belly.

Those long fingers closed around his cock.

"Damn it, Hel…" Forgetting cooperation, he reared up.

In silent reproach, she lifted her hand away.

"Damn it," he repeated in a lower voice, lying back.

"So nice to deal with a clever man," she purred. She kissed him, but pulled away before the kiss found a life of its own.

"I'm not feeling clever," he muttered, anchoring his hands in the cushions so he didn't grab her.

He'd never been sure how far she meant to take her quest to conquer him. Now he had his answer. To the edge of endurance and beyond.

"Shall I touch you again?" she murmured.

If she didn't, he'd bloody well explode. "Yes."

Once more, her hand closed around his dick. She sounded as if she was making notes. "I find your body so fascinating. It's so hard and hot."

Before he could muster a response to that, she began to slide her hand up and down. Her clumsy caresses were astonishingly arousing. He gritted his teeth against spilling like an overenthusiastic schoolboy.

She stopped.

Why in Hades did she stop?

He forced his eyes open to find her observing him with a troubled expression. "Am I doing something wrong? You don't look very comfortable."

"Squeeze. Tighter."

As if he'd given her the solution to a mathematical problem, she nodded.

Her touch became more confident. He found it impossible to look away. She concentrated so intently, it was like the future of the world relied on her success.

One thumb rubbed across the glistening moisture at his tip. Heat seared him, and he started to shake the way he shook when he was ill.

She must take him into her body soon. Her heavy eyes betrayed how this slow seduction excited her. Her nipples had hardened into rosy points. The air was thick with the scent of burning coals, aroused male, sweet female musk.

His heart slammed to a quivering stop as she shifted. She was sliding down to kneel between his outspread legs. *Surely she wouldn't...*

Helena shot him a smile all bright devilry, and dipped her head to take him in her mouth.

CHAPTER ELEVEN

*W*hen the hot, wet suction of Helena's mouth surrounded him, West went taut as a violin string. Furious pleasure blasted him. He groaned and struggled to cling to reality.

He couldn't let her do this. She must hate it.

Her tongue flickered over the head, and he shuddered. He needed every ounce of willpower to reach down and bury his hands in her wild hair.

"No, Hel…" he gasped. "Stop."

With a leisurely movement that threatened to hurl him to Kingdom Come, she raised her head and regarded him with puzzled dark eyes. "Don't you like it? Crewe did."

Good God, the last thing he needed to hear right now was that swine's name. "I don't want you to do anything you don't want to."

Which was an outright lie. He wanted her mouth on

him more than he wanted to live another five minutes. When she licked her lips, he bit back another groan.

"Crewe tried to make me do this, but I found it too revolting."

Disappointment cramped his gut. Although what else could he expect? "Then why?"

"Because this is *you*. Because I want to give you pleasure. Because I feel no shame in what we do together. With you, this is almost...pure." Uncertainty darkened her eyes. "If you can bear it."

A grunt of wry laughter. "You're bringing a thousand fantasies to life."

Helena's expression filled with incredulous delight. "Really?"

"Really." Still his inconvenient conscience wouldn't let him finish there. Dear Lord, he earned his place in heaven today. He hoped the Recording Angel was listening in. "Promise you'll stop if it becomes too—"

Heavy eyelids descended. "I like it."

The devils prancing about in his heart settled. Her willingness made no sense in any universe he inhabited, but he couldn't doubt she meant it. "Then by all means, continue."

An excited huff of laughter escaped her. With one hand, she gathered her hair behind her neck, while the other circled the thick base of his cock.

Control became more ragged when she lowered over him. He clawed at the cushions and prayed for fortitude through an interval of excruciating pleasure before she found her rhythm. When she did, she rocketed him into a volatile new world of heat and sensuality.

That fiendish tongue prolonged the torture, and she stroked his balls in a caress that crashed through him like cannon fire. His breath emerged in guttural grunts. Every muscle strained toward climax. Every ounce of will kept him from surrendering.

Through the gathering storm, he remembered she was a fine lady. He couldn't lose himself in her mouth. Yet with every second, release rushed nearer.

Ignoring her rules, he plunged shaking hands into her hair. He had to stop her before it was too late. The words scraped out of his tight throat. "Helena, I'm too close."

She raised her head. "Give yourself to me."

The husky, urgent command smashed through him. His hands clenched in her hair. "You don't understand."

"Yes, I do."

Without waiting for an answer, she bowed her head and swept him into sizzling paradise. She squeezed his balls with exquisite pressure.

It was beyond bearing. He couldn't hold back. He wanted this too much.

With a drawn-out groan, West arched against the cushions and gave himself up to flooding ecstasy.

~

West's hoarse cry woke Helena from exhausted sleep. It was the dead of night, and her bed was shaking.

An earthquake?

She took a few disoriented seconds to realize that West was shivering and moving restlessly beside her. He'd kicked aside the covers, although the night was cold and the fire had burned down to hot coals.

"West?" She leaned over him and placed one hand on his bare shoulder. Dear Lord, he was bathed in sweat, and his skin burned under her touch. In the dark, she fumbled for her nightdress and dragged it over her head.

She should have seen this coming. He'd been quiet all evening. She'd wondered if the direction of their affair worried him. It certainly worried her.

During those tumultuous hours in the summer-house, they'd forged a profound connection. Profound, and troubling. As Helena fell further and further under West's spell, the prospect of living without him became unbearable.

What a fool she was to think she could emerge unchanged from such incendiary passion. Now the awkward question was where they went from here. She still shrank from marriage. But the prospect of sending him away in a few days left her desolate. She felt lost and confused, and unable to make her next step.

Tonight when he'd come to bed, he'd settled down with her in his arms and dropped into exhausted sleep. It had all felt horribly—wonderfully—matrimonial.

Even worse, nestling beside him in drowsy contentment, she had the oddest fancy that this was where she belonged.

She pulled the blankets up and smoothed the damp black hair back from his high forehead. "Hush, sweetheart. Shhh." She hardly noticed the endearment.

At least her touch brought him a measure of comfort. As the terrifying shaking eased, he opened his eyes. "Helena."

She caught his hand. "You're sick."

"Damn it. I'm sorry."

"Don't be a fool." She rose from the bed and lit a couple of candles, then almost wished she hadn't. West looked appalling. White and drawn, eyes sunk back in his face.

He took an unsteady breath. "I'll go."

"You can't be alone."

The shivering started again. "Staying here will cause a scandal."

"The others won't tell anyone."

"They mightn't." Strain plastered his skin to the bones of his face. "But there's a household full of servants who won't keep the news to themselves. With the wedding, they'll have plenty of visitors to tell."

"I don't care. Anyway, if the housemaids have eyes, they must know I haven't slept alone the last two nights." To think she'd once fretted about gossip. All that mattered now was West's health. "What can I do?"

"Help me back to my room. You don't have to nurse me."

She frowned. However brave his offer, it wasn't practical. He wasn't fit to stand, let alone wander the hallways. And her soul screamed denial at the idea of consigning him to another's care. "Maybe later," she said to head off an argument.

She might as well have saved her breath. His eyes turned opaque, and his teeth chattered. He obviously couldn't hear her.

How could he survive this? And he'd suffered these bouts for months. Helpless pity crushed her heart.

She fetched a glass of water and held him against her bosom while he tried to drink. Most of the water went over him, rather than down his throat. He was a big man, and even a strong woman like her struggled to support his weight.

"Cold, cold," he said over and over, while he fought to throw off the covers.

Increasingly worried, Helena sponged him down, speaking soothing nonsense. Her voice seemed to calm him, as she ran a damp cloth over his naked body, noting again how thin he was.

He raised a shaking hand. She set the bowl aside and took it.

"Helena." The sound was a whisper, although his grip was firm.

"I'm here, darling," she murmured.

"Help me back to my room."

"We won't make it." She cupped the side of his face, distraught that despite her efforts, his fever worsened.

"Let's try." He was becoming agitated.

"Very well."

Helena took both his hands and helped him to sit, trembling and sick, on the edge of the bed. She slid her shoulder under his arm. "Hold on to me."

Staggering, she got him up, but on the first step, he reeled.

"This is hopeless, West," she said, stumbling to keep him upright. "I'll get Silas."

And she'd send for a doctor, scandal be damned. Since she'd woken, she'd been afraid, but seeing strong, self-confident Vernon Grange unable to stand had her stomach twisting with terror.

She'd known he was ill. She'd seen for herself how the fever came upon him out of nowhere. But only now, when she battled alone against this enemy, did she understand that she might lose him.

Suddenly that seemed the worst blow fate could deal her. Crueler by far than an unhappy marriage.

How precious he was. How precious he'd always been.

If West lived, she didn't care if the whole county shunned her as a brazen trollop.

"No...Silas," he said, before retreating into the occasional grunt as she struggled to get him back into bed.

Leaning in, she kissed his hot forehead. "I'll be back in a moment."

She flung a dressing gown over her shoulders, grabbed a candle, and dashed out of the room. Once, she'd been glad that her rooms were in a separate wing. Then she'd been worried about keeping her affair with West a secret.

Now she'd declare her disgrace from the rooftops, if it brought him one scrap of relief. She cursed every yard of corridor stretching between her and help.

By the time she reached Silas's door, she was breathless. She pounded on it. "Blast you, Silas, wake up!"

Her brother took an eon to appear. "Helena? What the devil's got into you?"

"West is sick. I think he's going to die. Come quickly." Behind her brother, she saw Caro sitting up in bed and clutching the sheets to her bare breasts.

"Is it the fever again?" Caro asked.

"Yes. I'll go downstairs and send a servant for the doctor."

"No, you go with Silas. I'll organize Dr. Lawson."

"He looked fine at dinner," Silas said, coming out into the corridor and tying his dressing gown more securely.

"Well, he's not fine now." She grabbed her brother's hand and rushed back the way she'd come. "Hurry."

A mountainous man in a crimson dressing gown emerged from the shadows. "What's all this hubbub?"

"West's sick," Silas said to Anthony.

Fen appeared, too. "I thought he was quiet tonight. Has someone sent for a doctor?"

"Caro's rousing the servants," Silas said. "She'll have a groom off to the village in minutes."

They trooped toward Helena's room, but as they came to the wide landing above the main staircase, something tall and white stumbled out of the darkness.

"Silas?" the apparition rasped, weaving on the spot.

"West!" Helena cried out, darting forward and flinging her arm around his waist. Violent tremors shook his lean form. How he'd made it this far, she had no idea. "You should be in bed."

"Sleep…walking," he managed to say loudly enough for the others to hear, then despite all her efforts, his legs folded.

Anthony could move like lightning, it turned out. Before West hit the floor, the big man caught him.

"He's out cold." With characteristic competence, he hitched West up by the armpits.

"I'd be out cold, too, wandering the corridors on a February night in nothing but a sheet," Silas said, lifting West's bare feet.

Helena stepped away in favor of the men. In her anguish, she hadn't noticed that West was wrapped in a sheet, she guessed from her bed. He'd come to her in his evening clothes, but the intricacies of fashionable dress were clearly beyond him.

As was his ability to listen to a lecture. How on

earth could he put his health at risk over something as trivial as her reputation?

"We'll take him to his room," Silas said. "Hel's is too far away."

Caro called from below. "A groom's gone for Dr. Lawson. He should be here soon."

Silas and Anthony hauled the unconscious West away. Helena set off after them, but Fen caught her arm. "Come and wait with Caro and me."

"I don't want to leave him."

Fen's eyes were soft with compassion as she untangled Helena's fingers from the candlestick. "I know you don't, but it's better he's with Silas and Anthony when the doctor arrives."

Fen was right. West had gone to heroic efforts to preserve Helena's good name. The least she could do was ensure his work wasn't in vain. Mute with dread, she let her friend lead her downstairs.

CHAPTER TWELVE

*I*n the library, Fen poured Helena a brandy. With a trembling hand, she accepted the glass and collapsed onto a sofa. Across the room, a footman kneeled before the hearth, lighting the fire. The tall clock in the corner chimed three. It was bitterly cold, and Helena curled her bare toes into the carpet in search of warmth. She hadn't stopped to put slippers on when she'd rushed out of her room in a panic.

"Where's Caro?" Her voice was scratchy.

Fen crossed to the window and opened the curtains on a starlit night. "Probably doing her best to make West comfortable."

The footman rose and bowed to Helena. "Shall I arrange for refreshments, my lady?"

She mustered a smile. "Yes, please, John. The doctor

will want something to eat when he's finished, I imagine."

"Very good, my lady."

"Please pass my apologies to the staff for the interrupted night. I'll come and speak to everyone once we know what's happening."

"We all wish Lord West well. He's always been a favorite downstairs."

Another reminder of how her life was entwined with West's. "Thank you."

Once John left, she placed her empty glass on a side table and stood. "I'm going upstairs. If Caro's with him, why can't I be there, too?"

Fen turned away from staring outside. "Helena, there's nothing you can do."

"He might want me."

"If he asks for you, Silas will tell us."

Regret and self-recrimination settled cold and heavy in her belly. She had no standing in West's life. A wife could attend a sickbed. While she was nothing but a childhood friend and temporary mistress, damn it.

She began to pace, seeking some relief in movement. "Where is that doctor?"

Fen watched her with a troubled expression. "West has survived every bout of fever so far, Helena. He's bad for a few days, then he's well again. You saw it yourself this week."

That was before she'd found ecstasy in his arms—and the heavenly peace of lying beside him after passion was sated. That was before the idea of a world without him sent her into an agony of fear. "This time is different."

Fen didn't ask why it was different, but then, Fen, unlike Caro, was renowned for her tact. Instead, she crossed the room and hugged Helena. "Don't torment yourself."

Briefly she rested in Fen's embrace. Then she broke free to pace again. "I can't help it."

Fenella sank into her usual chair. "He'll be up and about, and ready to dance at the wedding."

"You can't be sure." Wringing her hands, Helena quartered the floor. She paused when a door banged in the wind. "What's that?"

"I assume it's the doctor arriving." Fen reached for her embroidery. She wore a pink silk wrap, and she'd thought to put slippers on her feet. With her golden hair flowing around her shoulders and her lovely face soft with lack of sleep, she looked like a young girl.

Around them, Helena heard the unmistakable sounds of the house coming alive. "I must see him."

Fen placed a careful stitch. "And say what?"

Fen was right. What could she say? If she'd accepted West's proposal, she'd have a wife's rights.

But she was nobody.

She returned to the couch and stared into the distance, her mind awash with excruciating pictures of West dying without her saying goodbye. Or thank you.

John returned and set out the tea service. Helena

appreciated the warm drink, although her stomach revolted at the sandwiches and pastries. Mrs. Ballard, the cook, had done a marvelous job at this unfriendly hour.

After he left, silence fell. Helena supposed she should go upstairs and dress. If she meant to waylay the doctor and wheedle a visit to the sickroom, she'd rather not be wearing her nightdress.

Caro came in, looking tired. "Is that tea?"

Helena rose to pour. "What news?"

"He's in and out of consciousness. The doctor says the fever is taking its course."

The teapot rattled against the cup as Helena's hand shook. "What the devil does that mean?"

Caro accepted the tea with a weary smile. "That the fever is taking its course, I expect. Oh, lovely. Ham sandwiches. Ridiculous to be hungry in the middle of the night, but I am."

"To Hades with your hunger," Helena exploded. "West could be dying up there."

Caro eyed her with disapproval. "He's come through before."

Fenella sipped her tea. "Hel, for heaven's sake, take a deep breath and sit down. It won't do anyone a morsel of good if you go to pieces."

Helena slumped onto the sofa and brushed the heavy fall of hair back from her face. "I'm making rather a fool of myself, aren't I?"

"We all go a little mad when we're in love." Fen's voice was gentle. "It's nice to see you're not immune."

"In love?" she asked, shocked. Then so many things that in her panic had gone unnoticed crashed down on her like a huge wave. Her tone sharpened. "You know. You both know."

"That you and West are head over heels? Of course we do," Fen said comfortably.

Of course they did.

When she'd battered at their bedroom door, neither Caro nor Silas had evinced a shred of surprise that Helena was the one who knew West was ill. Nor for that matter, had Fen or Anthony.

And Silas had headed toward her room without asking where West was.

She frowned. "How did you know we'd reached an…understanding?"

Which was a mealy-mouthed way to describe their transcendent hours together. She didn't pursue the head over heels remark. Her feelings were too confused right now for her to mount a suitable defense.

Caro rolled her eyes. "Where do I start? I know we're both distracted, but we're not blind. You and West were so busy, trying not to look at each other. I saw the marks on your neck the other morning, despite that stylish high collar. And the two of you came in yesterday afternoon looking distinctly heavy-eyed, you naughty pair. Not to mention that for the last few days, your acid wit has verged on sweet. Not a sarcastic remark to be heard."

Helena shifted uncomfortably. "How revolting."

"I think it's lovely," Fenella said.

"You would," Caro said, casting her an unimpressed glance.

Helena spread her hands. "Why didn't you say something? Fen's the soul of delicacy, but discretion isn't your way."

Caro was unoffended. "Because if we did, you'd dig in your heels, and do your best to ruin everything out of sheer contrariness."

Helena scowled at her closest friends. "You make me sound blindly obstinate."

"When you're always the voice of reason," Caro said, taking a fair stab at sarcasm herself.

"So now your secret's out, what do you plan to do?" Fen asked. "Has he proposed?"

"You've got marriage on the brain. West and I are taking a few days to scratch a mutual itch, then we go back to being mostly polite strangers."

"If you say so," Fen said.

"Really," Helena said.

"That seems sensible," Caro said.

"I mean it."

Fenella returned to her embroidery. "Helena, nobody's arguing with you."

Helena made a disgruntled sound and leaned back

in her chair. "I have this awful feeling you're both trying to manage me."

"Wouldn't dream of it, Hel. You're more than capable of steering your own life," Caro said cheerfully. "You don't need us."

"That's right." She winced as she heard the unnecessary emphasis she gave the words.

So did Caro. Her lips curved into a smirk.

Helena's scowl deepened. "Don't you dare laugh at me, Caroline Beaumont."

"I wouldn't be so bold." Her smirk became a giggle.

"Caro," Helena said in a warning tone.

Caro returned her cup to its saucer. "It's just…" She took a breath to steady her voice. It didn't make a noticeable difference. "I know West is frightfully ill, and it's been a dreadful night, and you're worried sick about him, but…" Another gurgle of laughter escaped. "But I can't help seeing Lord West staggering out of the shadows, wearing only a sheet. It was like…like Caesar's ghost had come to haunt the house."

She went off into whoops, and Fen started to laugh, too. Helena glowered at them. How could they laugh when West was so sick?

Then she recalled that odd moment, horrendous at the time, now strangely comic. She remembered West's clever, but unlikely claim that he was sleepwalking. And she burst into laughter herself.

❧

The morning of Caro and Silas's wedding dawned bright with sunshine, as if even nature blessed this union. As West dressed, he glanced out the window at the pristine beauty of fields and hills. It had snowed, and pure sparkling white changed the Nash estate from a familiar landscape into the setting for a fairy tale.

As soon as he regained his senses, he'd sent for his valet from London. The man fussed around him now, smoothing out any wrinkles bold enough to mar the perfection of his dark blue coat and cream silk waistcoat.

This bout of fever had been bad, and chafing at the inactivity, he'd spent most of the last four days in bed. He'd managed to make it downstairs to dinner the last two nights, but the effort had exhausted him.

Enforced rest had left him with far too much time to think. And the thoughts hadn't been congenial. At times, he'd wished he was still out of his head.

West had always enjoyed rude good health. When he'd first contracted this damned malady, he'd assumed it would prove a brief inconvenience, then become an unpleasant memory.

That, it turned out, had been optimistic ignorance. For six months now, he'd suffered regular bouts of appalling physical misery. After this latest attack, he couldn't avoid the bleak fact that his illness had become a permanent part of his life.

And he loathed it.

"Am I discommoding your lordship?" Cooper asked nervously, straightening West's snowy white cuffs.

Distracted from gloomy musings, West glanced at the valet. "No. Why?"

"You looked rather fierce, sir."

West's thoughts had trended toward grimness since he'd collapsed into Anthony Townsend's arms, wearing nothing but a sheet. "No. I'm fine."

Except he wasn't.

As he stood before the mirror, his legs wobbled, and he felt alarmingly lightheaded. But damn it, he'd get through this wedding ceremony, or he might as well put a bullet through his brain.

The ancient village church was packed, and a crowd formed outside, despite the snow. Lining the pews were local friends, privileged villagers, and various Nashes who had arrived over the last few days. Silas was well loved, and everyone was delighted that he and his bride were so devoted.

West and Silas had driven up in an open carriage. Silas claimed he wanted to arrive in style, but West knew it was to save him from making the short walk. He'd wanted to snarl at his friend that he wasn't a bloody invalid. Until he admitted the unpalatable truth that even such an easy stroll was beyond him.

Now they stood at the altar while the last of the

congregation found their places. Fen and Anthony came in. The first time he'd seen them together, they'd seemed an incongruous couple. Delicate Fenella and her rough, gruff shipping magnate.

Now West was convinced she couldn't have found anyone better. She looked lovely in a pink velvet gown trimmed with swansdown. She'd always been pretty, but love transformed her to radiant beauty.

Accompanying them were two half-grown boys. The fair one he recognized as Fenella's son Brandon, while the dark one had such a look of his uncle that he must be Carey Townsend, Anthony's ward.

Reluctantly his gaze moved past Fen and Anthony to where Helena paused in the doorway to speak to an elderly cousin. Every muscle tightened in forbidden longing.

Helena. His joy. His torment. His obsession. The impossible fate.

Since his illness, he'd seen little of her. Deliberately.

She'd dared propriety to visit his sickroom, but he'd ensured they weren't alone. He'd sensed her increasing frustration, but he didn't yet trust himself to do the right thing. At least when she had him cornered in a bedroom.

As soon as he could hold a pen, he'd asked the reliably discreet Cooper to deliver a note. The message had promised a discussion after the wedding. Once the house emptied of all those hawk-eyed relatives, and

West had the strength to say what he must. For her sake.

The note had prompted an immediate visit. He should have known it would. But he'd pretended to be asleep, and she'd retreated in defeat. She'd tried again, of course. His Helena wasn't one to accept the first setback. But the guests filling the house hampered her movements, and the doctor had insisted on constant nursing for West while he recovered.

These stratagems only put off the evil hour. He'd have to talk to her soon. It was unfair to leave her dangling.

Although a clever creature like Helena must already know something had changed.

West was determined to meet her in a public place, with no chance of laying his hands on her. Because if he did, every scruple would fly out the window. When Helena was within reach, he didn't trust his ability to master his baser urges.

Today or tomorrow, he'd set her free. Despite all her claims to emotional detachment, he knew she wouldn't thank him now. However, he was sure she'd thank him in time.

Poor comfort, but all he could muster at this moment.

With her usual eye-catching saunter, Helena moved into the body of the church. In all this crowd, he saw only her. And damn it, if she didn't instantly look over the sea of heads toward him. Despite everything, heat blasted him.

Heat. Sorrow. And something else that he forbade a name.

Before he made an ass of himself, he broke the connection and turned to stare at the flower-bedecked altar. Silas's greenhouses had come up trumps again.

But the image of Helena, tall, elegant and somehow tragically alone, despite her clamorous family about her, remained burned on his eyes. She wore crimson, and her shining hair was bundled up beneath an absurd confection of feathers and ribbons and pearls.

"What the devil is the matter with you?" Silas growled out of the side of his mouth. "I will not have my groomsman looking like a bilious seagull."

He raised his eyebrows. "A bilious seagull?"

"Yes. The beaky nose makes the resemblance unmistakable." Silas released a hiss of exasperation. "Damn it, it's my wedding. Try and act like it's a jolly occasion. Your problems with my dashed troublesome sister will keep."

Silas had a point. "Sorry, old man."

But Silas had fallen silent, transfixed by what he saw at the church door. The organist started to play as West turned. Silas's pretty, tawny-haired sister Amy stepped forward, wearing a fashionable light blue gown. Caro followed a few paces behind.

West caught his breath. Caro had always been lovely, but today she dazzled. She wore a gown of rich gold silk, and her deep brown hair was braided in a crown around her head. She carried a bouquet of spring flowers. Lily of the valley, snowdrops and violets, twined about with ivy to symbolize fidelity. Befitting a woman of her originality, no man walked by her side. She gave herself to Silas with an independent will and a loving heart.

She looked proud and happy, and transfigured by love. As if the angels agreed, the sun chose that moment to stream through the stained glass windows and bathe her in brilliant light.

"You're a lucky man, old son," he said to Silas.

"More than I deserve." Silas smiled at his bride. She smiled back, and misery punched West. He didn't resent his friend's good fortune, but he knew that he'd never look across a crowded church to see the woman he wanted walking toward him.

With a rustle, the congregation rose. The vicar stepped forward with the prayer book in his hands. West packed away his selfish concerns so he could watch his best friend pledge himself to the woman he loved.

CHAPTER THIRTEEN

*I*n the commotion after the ceremony, Helena lost track of West. Which was something of a miracle, given she'd been burningly conscious of him from the moment she entered the church. Her heart had slammed to a stop at the sight of him waiting at the altar, tall and handsome in his blue coat.

Tall and handsome, and drawn and tired. Today he appeared ten years older than the man she'd seduced in the summerhouse.

Despite his best attempts to avoid looking at her—honestly, he must know the game was up when it came to hiding their liaison—a thread of fire had connected them. But as Silas and Caro left for Woodley Park in a barouche garlanded with ribbons and hothouse flowers, she glanced around the rice-strewn churchyard and realized that West had disappeared.

Fear stirred. He'd been so ill. Had he collapsed somewhere, and in all the hullabaloo, nobody noticed?

Berating herself, she retreated from the thinning crowd—Silas had laid on a celebration for the villagers at the tavern, while his friends and family walked back to the house for the wedding breakfast.

One last check of the area. No West.

She started her hunt in the church, but only saw the vicar's wife collecting hymn books. Helena shivered and wrapped her arms around herself. Without the press of warm bodies, the old stone building was cold.

Where on earth was West? Had he slipped away to the house ahead of everyone else? After the ceremony, carriages had driven the old and infirm up to the breakfast. But she couldn't see West, no matter how ill, admitting that he fell into that category.

She emerged into the day, blinking at the glare of sun on snow. The villagers had cleared the road, and the area in front of the church, but white blanketed everything else.

What a perfect winter day for a perfect winter wedding. Caro and Silas's transparent happiness had brought a tear to even unsentimental Helena Wade's eye. Her brother and his bride deserved every ounce of their joy.

Helena made her way around the church, thankful anew for the villagers' hard work. Her fur-lined half-boots were a stylish take on seasonal footwear, but they weren't up to wading through snow. She shaded her eyes and looked over the graves—although why West would choose to wander among tombstones today of all days, she couldn't imagine.

Still no sign of him. He must have left without her noticing. Which seemed dashed odd.

Nettled and still worried, she turned to retrace her steps, and caught sight of a pair of long—and familiar —legs. They extended across the entrance to the stone porch outside the vestry.

Propelled by a mixture of relief and concern, she hurried forward. "West? Aren't you well?"

During the ceremony, he'd looked pale and serious. She suspected iron will alone had kept him standing.

"Helena." He didn't look up as she appeared in the doorway. "My day is complete."

She flinched as foreboding settled heavy in her stomach. The words might be flattering. His tone was not. He sounded like the drawling, sardonic rake she'd so disliked in London.

He'd removed his hat and set it on the bench beside him. She bit back the urge to insist he put it on against the cold. The last thing he'd want was her fussing about his health.

"Are you all right?" Needing the support, she set a shaky hand on the stone archway. His closed expression deterred her from touching him.

His illness might explain this cool reception, she supposed. Although she couldn't help feeling something more personal lay behind his reserve.

He concentrated on the flagstoned floor. "Of course I am."

She set a hand on her hip. "Then why are you brooding in here?"

"Just catching my breath. You go ahead. I'll be there soon."

She struggled to hide how his dismissal stung. "You've been avoiding me."

At last, he lifted his eyes. The green was flat as she'd never seen it. "Yes, I have."

She was surprised at the ready admission. Surprised, puzzled—and hurt. "Why?"

Impatience lengthened the lips that had kissed her into a frenzy. "Because there's something I need to say. And I don't want to spoil Silas's wedding for you."

She stiffened her spine and raised her chin. "Well, that's damned considerate of you."

He shook his glossy head. As if anchoring himself in place, he hooked his gloved hands over the edge of the oak bench. "We need privacy, and no likelihood of interruption."

Worse and worse. Sick apprehension knotted her stomach. The last time he'd wanted privacy and no interruptions, he'd sent her to paradise and back. The contrast with today was chilling.

She clutched trembling hands together at her waist, before deliberately separating them and lowering them to her sides. His distant attitude scraped tattered holes in her heart, but she was a fighter, not a helpless victim. "Don't leave me hanging."

A muscle flickered in his lean cheek. "The vicar's still inside the church, and we're expected at the house. I'm due to make a speech, if you recall."

She set her jaw and marched into the small space, despite West's silent warning to keep out. "The vicar and his wife left a few minutes ago. You don't have to do your speech until the end of the breakfast. And you're not weaseling out of telling me what's going on, even if we sit here until Christmas."

He sighed again. "People will talk."

"Let them." With legs that felt like string, she sank onto the narrow bench opposite West. It was colder in his dank hideout than it was outside in the sun. "What's wrong?"

He smiled with grudging fondness—and a regret that sliced at her like a razor. "Always ready to rush in where angels fear to tread."

She didn't smile back—after all, he hadn't given her much of a smile in the first place. "Are you angry because our friends now know we're...involved?"

"No. Although that doesn't mean I want the whole bloody county knowing our business."

She leaned back on the clammy medieval stone. She didn't understand what was happening. Which was strange when she and West had shared such an uncanny connection.

But whatever troubled him, he needed to know that the game had changed.

"West, I will marry you."

Whatever reaction she expected, it wasn't the one she got. For a blistering instant, he stared at her in absolute horror. Then he tipped his head against the wall and laughed.

His sour amusement bounced around the stone walls like mistuned bells. Devastated, angry, bewildered, Helena surged to her feet and glared at him. Her hands formed fists at her sides, although she knew she couldn't thump a man only hours out of his sickbed.

"What the devil is wrong with you?"

He stopped laughing and leveled cold eyes upon her. Shocked, distraught, she stumbled back onto the bench.

His lips twisted. "Do any two people in history have worse timing than you and me?"

That didn't sound good. That didn't sound good at all.

Dread colder than the snow outside oozed down her spine. "What do you mean?" she asked in a reedy voice.

The humor, however bitter, drained from his face. He looked weary and desolate.

She wasn't a stupid woman, although right now, she feared she'd been fatally stupid about West. Before he spoke, she knew what he was going to say. Although she still couldn't fathom how everything could shift in mere days.

"I mean that I've changed my mind." His deep voice was toneless. He didn't sound at all like the man who had slept by her side and caressed her until she cried out in ecstasy. "I won't marry you, Helena."

Although his manner already hinted at that answer, she recoiled. Having her heart crushed beneath his boot heel hurt like the very devil. Tears pricked her eyes, but she blinked them back. She wouldn't cry. It would be too humiliating.

She couldn't help but remember the afternoon in the summerhouse. She'd never trusted anyone so deeply. She'd never felt so happy.

Her nails bit into her palms as she struggled for control. Crewe had taught her all about disappointment and loneliness and shame. This should be more of the same.

Except it wasn't.

Because she'd soon realized that her so-called love for Crewe was only adolescent romanticism, allied with his dedicated pursuit of her—and her dowry. Whereas her bond with West was real.

Or at least she'd believed it was.

Mustering her ragged courage, she squared her shoulders. "Is that all you've got to say?"

"Yes." That muscle in his cheek continued its erratic dance. He looked uncomfortable and miserable and strained.

Which also struck her as strange. This couldn't be the first time a libertine like West had dismissed an incompatible lover. He should be better at it.

Her brain scurried for explanations. Only one reason occurred to her, and it made her feel like vomiting. "Is it…"

Helena broke off. It seemed blasphemous to say the words outside a church, but she had to know. When she'd taken him into her mouth, she'd felt so free and brave. But men were bizarre creatures. Perhaps he saw her actions in a different light.

She steeled herself to ask the question. "Did I give you a disgust of me, when I—"

His features tightened in dismay, and he reached out convulsively. But he stopped before making contact and curled his hands over the bench again. "No. Good God, no. That was one of the most glorious experiences of my life."

At least he no longer sounded like a bored roué rejecting an unpromising courtesan. She stared into his face, and at last her sharp mind kicked into its usual efficient action. Whatever lay behind this lunatic decision, it wasn't because he'd tired of her.

Just now he'd betrayed himself. She'd glimpsed hunger and longing, and something that looked very much like self-hatred.

Now his expression was shuttered, and he stared over her right shoulder as if the old stonework was the most fascinating thing he'd ever seen.

She sucked in a breath of freezing air and forced herself to think, instead of feel. Feeling wouldn't help her here.

Four days ago, everything between them had been perfect. So whatever the problem, it had arisen since he'd collapsed with fever.

Helena strove for calmness. "If you don't want to marry me, we'll do as you suggested, and go on as lovers."

That caught his attention. He stared at her as if she was mad. "That's not possible."

West seemed determined to make an operatic drama out of their affair. She was equally determined to drag him back to reality. And the reality was that they belonged together, even if she'd taken far too long to admit that.

"Why not?" She shrugged with manufactured insouciance. "Although we may run into trouble when you choose a bride. After all, you need an heir."

Deep lines ran between his nose and mouth. "I doubt I'll ever marry."

She frowned as explanations for his behavior, none related to wanting to move on from her, hurtled through her mind. She wasn't experienced with dalliance, but nor was she a fool. She couldn't help remembering a man barely able to crawl who had struggled out of his sickbed to protect her good name.

"That seems a pity." Holding West's gaze, she rose

and, daring the bristling hostility, sat beside him. "What about the title?"

He slid away, but she hadn't left him much room to maneuver. "I have cousins aplenty."

"That's a mercy, then," she said with assumed cheerfulness. She inched along the seat until her hip bumped his.

He eyed her warily, winged brows lowered in displeasure. "Must you sit so close?"

"It's cold." She caught his gloved hand in hers.

"So why not head up to the house?" He vibrated with tension, but didn't break free. "There's nothing for you here."

How wrong could a man be? "I'm waiting for you to tell me why you wanted me one day, and you can't abide me the next. It doesn't seem like you."

Despite lack of encouragement, her senses expanded to his nearness. The lemon soap he used. Beneath that, the musky scent of his skin. The warmth of his body. She'd felt glacially cold when he'd tried to send her away, but now frail hope warmed her blood.

Dear God, don't let her be wrong.

"That's rakes for you," he said.

If he meant to sound like the heartless debauchee she'd once believed him to be, he failed. She raised his hand and rubbed her cheek against his knuckles. "Maybe, but I know now I misjudged you all these years. You're a man of steady affections, unshakable loyalty, and the highest honor."

This time he did wrench away, despite her best efforts to cling to him. He stumbled to his feet and stared at her angrily. "What's this, Hel?"

As she studied him, tentative hope firmed, and settled hard and sure inside her. "I'm saying I know your game."

He scowled. "This is no game. Our affair is over. I'm sending you away."

She glowered back. "I won't go."

He flinched as though she'd hit him. "Have you no pride?"

It was her turn for an unamused laugh. "Of course. Too much." She shot him a straight look. "But unlike you, I'm not stupid with pride."

His expression turned shifty, which bolstered her optimism that she was on the right track. "You're talking utter rubbish."

She folded her gloved hands in her lap and fixed him with an unwavering regard. "No, you are. You should know me by now, West. I'm steadfast and true. For pity's sake, I remained faithful to that swine Crewe. Now I've chosen you, and I won't be fobbed off." Impatience roughened her tone. "As if your illness makes a shred of difference to my affection."

More than affection. But while she was brave, she wasn't brave enough to set her whole heart out before him. Not when she still wasn't sure whether he meant to surrender, or crush all her chances of happiness. And all his chances, too, the stiff-necked wretch.

A long, prickling silence extended.

Suspense tightened her belly until bile rose in her throat. Was she wrong? Had she pushed him too far?

Then he dragged in a shuddering breath. He slumped as the resistance drained out of him. And with it, the rage-fueled vigor.

Relief flooded her, and she leaped to her feet, helping him back to the bench. "Should I fetch someone?"

"A keeper to take you away and lock you up," he said, although the words lacked venom. He leaned against her, heavy and trembling and dear.

She wasn't complaining. At least they'd bridged the cruel distance. She turned her head to kiss the ruffled dark hair. "Make your heroic declaration of self-denial. Then I can argue it away, and we can get on with the rest of our lives."

Despite physical discomfort, a grunt of laughter escaped him. "You're bloody sure of yourself."

"That's your fault." Her embrace tightened. "You make me feel like a goddess."

"I should have been more careful," he muttered, but his arm snaked around her waist to draw her closer. "It's all very well to sound so confident. I saw doctors in Russia, and again in London. These fevers could go on for the rest of my life. There's no cure. I might get better, but it's quite possible I won't."

She'd been right about what troubled him. Relief made her dizzy, but she stiffened her shoulders against any weakness. The fight wasn't over yet. "So like a gallant fool, you decided to fall on your sword, and throw me to the wolves for good measure?"

He shifted to level somber green eyes on her. "You deserve my best."

Heaven save her from stubborn masculine pride. "And it didn't occur to you to share these ramshackle ideas?"

"I know your stalwart soul, Helena. I've known it all my life. You'd insist on standing by me."

"Now who's sure of himself?"

"I know you've...become attached. It seemed easier to let you go back to thinking I'm a worthless cad."

"Easier for whom?"

"Hating me helped you cope with Crewe's betrayals. I thought it might help again this time." Obstinacy squared his jaw. She realized with a sinking feeling that she hadn't won yet, although victory hovered close. "I can't bear to be a burden on you."

"So your vanity is more important than my happiness?"

"Vanity?" he snapped, sounding much more like himself.

Fear that even now, she still might fail, added an edge to her voice. A wonderful future opened up before them. She could see that so clearly. Why in Hades couldn't he?

"Yes. Vanity. I don't care if you're ill—oh, that's not right, of course I care—but it doesn't change my feelings. In the past days, you've brought me alive. Surely you know that." Tears stung her eyes, and this time she didn't force them back. "For heaven's sake, West, don't let your conceit shut me away in the dark."

"I was right—you do intend to stand by me. Blast you, I won't have it. I won't tie you to a wreck of a man."

"You're not a wreck of a man." A tear trickled down her cheek. How things had changed. Once he'd been so certain, and she'd been the one to hold out. "You're everything I want."

He stared at her in disbelief. "A week ago, you couldn't stand the sight of me."

"Well, now I can't go on without you. If you're intent on self-sacrifice, be self-sacrificing by my side. I'm not the easiest person in the world." She yielded the very last of her own pride. "Lover or wife, I don't care which. As long as we stay together."

A familiar mulish expression settled on his features. "No. I want to marry you."

More relief rose to choke her. She caught his intense, dark face between her hands and met eyes still brimming with uncertainty. "Then don't consign us both to a lonely life, just because you sometimes get the shakes."

He studied her. "Helena, I'm trying to do the right thing."

She dredged up a smile. "Then make an honest

woman of me. Really, Lord West, have you no scruples?"

Reluctant amusement tugged at his lips. "More than I ever realized. But you seem to have talked me out of most of them."

Closing her eyes, she sent a thankful prayer heavenward. She was terrifyingly aware of how close she'd come to losing him. "Really?"

"Really." The clumsy eagerness in his kiss showed as nothing else could that he was hers at last.

By the time he raised his head, she was befuddled and happy and shaking. Sniffing, she fumbled for a handkerchief in the satin reticule tied to her wrist.

"My dear Lady Crewe—" With difficulty, West shifted out of her arms and dropped to one knee before her.

Immediately she forgot what she was looking for. "Get up, West. That stone's too cold for you."

Despite her efforts to avoid him, he caught her hands. "Don't tell me you're going to be a nagging wife."

"Probably." She tried to break free. "I'll take the romantic proposal as read."

"No, you won't."

"For a decrepit ruin, you're very highhanded," she grumbled.

"You had your chance to run, and you didn't take it." His tight grip contradicted the humor. "My dear Lady Crewe—"

"You don't have to—"

"Yes, I do. Now be quiet and listen, curse you." His voice lowered to a velvety sincerity that made her tremble. "My dear Lady Crewe, I've long admired your beauty and kindness." He ignored her soft snort. "You are everything a man could want in a lifelong partner. I'll count myself the most fortunate of men if you accept me as your husband."

"I will," she said quickly.

"There's more."

She leaned down and kissed him. She'd expected resistance, but his mouth was eager. When she raised her head, her heart overflowed with happiness. "I don't need pretty words."

"Yes, you do." He raised her hands to his lips. "Helena, I'm not the perfect choice." He ignored the emphatic shake of her head, disagreeing with him. "Life will send us challenges. But you're the bravest and best woman I know, and I swear I'll cherish you until the day I die."

Oh, dear. A lump settled in Helena's throat, and moisture turned her vision misty. She should have found that handkerchief while she had the chance.

"Maybe I do need pretty words after all." She curled her fingers around his and struggled for the answer he deserved. "West, I pledge myself to you. I'll be proud to be your wife. Nobody has ever made me as happy as you have today."

This time the kiss lasted much longer, and ended in

the two of them entwined on the narrow bench. West no longer objected to her crowding him.

When he tucked her under his chin, she'd never felt so safe in her life. "The others will be pleased that we've made up our difficulties."

Helena gave a gurgle of laughter. "I have a suspicion they already know. My fellow Dashing Widows have an uncanny ability to sniff out a wedding in the wind."

"Now the Dashing Widows will all be cherished wives." Despite the wedding breakfast, he seemed content to linger in the shadowy porch. "Will you miss your wild ways, my darling?"

"My dear Lord West, how very wrong you are." She raised her head to meet his glowing eyes. "My dashing days have only just begun."

CHAPTER FOURTEEN

*W*est stood behind Helena on the steps of Woodley Park. Below them, Silas and Caro stepped into their traveling carriage in a flurry of farewells. But West's attention wasn't on his best friend and his bride. Instead his thoughts dwelled on the glorious woman who had at last consented to be his wife. His younger self had been wiser than his years when he'd set his sights on Silas's pretty sister.

How miraculous that in such a short space, despair could transform to joy. He'd been convinced that he was a hopeless invalid with nothing to offer her. And these last days with her had confirmed something he'd always known—that Helena deserved the best of everything.

While he mightn't be the best, he swore by everything he held holy that he'd do his best by her. Her hope was contagious. He felt better already.

By God, he'd beat this damned fever. He had something to live for now.

He stepped closer to catch the drift of her scent. Damn him if this surreptitious connection didn't give him an illicit thrill.

She cast him a quick glance, one knowing flash of bright, black eyes. Under cover of crimson skirts, her fingers tangled with his. Odd that her presence lent his soul such peace. She wasn't by nature a peaceful woman.

Of course if he announced their betrothal, there would be no need for subterfuge. An engaged couple holding hands might rouse interest but little disapproval, especially on such a romantic occasion. But this was Caro and Silas's day, however much West longed to shout hallelujahs and turn somersaults. He'd have the banns called next Sunday, but for now, his betrothal remained a delicious secret between Helena and him.

He leaned forward. "Can you slip away?"

She didn't look back, but her grip on his hand tightened. "Once I've made an appearance at the staff dinner, and farewelled the guests leaving today. Any family staying on can amuse themselves this afternoon, I'm sure."

"Come to my room."

"Someone will see."

"Not if they're all cuddled up in their own rooms."

"What about Amy?"

She wouldn't see his smug smile. "Ah, I've planned a treat for your inquisitive little sister. She's got an appointment at Shelton Abbey to talk to my agent about crop rotation."

Helena muffled a laugh. Not well enough. Her Great Aunt Agnes cast her a curious glance. "How Machiavellian. She'll be in alt. The poor fellow won't get away until midnight."

"Suits me." West inhaled her fragrance and felt her shiver with awareness. "I've missed you."

Helena directed a sharp eye at her elderly relative as she murmured, "Give me an hour."

"An hour will feel like eternity."

The familiar wry smile twisted her lips. "Goodness me, West. Are you sure you're feeling better? That doesn't sound like you at all."

He shrugged, unashamed of his ardor. "You've rumbled my secret. Under my rakish manners, I'm a sentimental fellow, my darling."

With visible reluctance, Great Aunt Agnes shifted her attention to Caro and Silas, who waved as their carriage rolled down the drive. But West predicted when he announced his betrothal, few would be caught unawares. Great Aunt Agnes was an inveterate gossip.

With everyone's backs turned, West dared to lift Helena's fingers to his lips. "Don't be too long, sweetheart."

～

At the soft click of his bedroom door, West sprang from the chair where he'd been trying to read. Trying and failing. How could printed words occupy him, when he waited in a lather of impatience for Helena?

The moment she stepped inside, he caught her up against him for a famished kiss. Fumbling to shut the door, he pressed her back until she bumped into the wooden panels.

He was starved for her, and still not quite convinced that they'd won through to a happy ending. Only this morning, he'd been sure she was lost to him forever. The few kisses outside the church hadn't come near to quenching his mighty need.

She kissed him back with brazen enthusiasm. It seemed he wasn't alone in craving more than kisses. When he'd come upstairs, he'd removed his coat and shoes. Now her frantic hands tore away his neck cloth and waistcoat.

In between kisses, she gasped out a breathless explanation. "I'm sorry I took so long. Great Aunt Agnes cornered me in the drawing room. She definitely knows something's up."

West tilted his hips forward. "Something is definitely...up."

"That's a terrible joke." But she moved closer, sending the blood crashing through his veins.

"You laughed. I heard you." That low, alluring chuckle always set every nerve in his body jumping.

For the first time in years, she sounded carefree.

"Only because I took pity on you. Seeing you've been ill, and all."

"I'm feeling *much* better." He stepped back to admire the lovely creature he'd captured for himself. "Pretty dress. Take it off."

Helena offered her back. "Unlace me. I didn't wear this with quick seduction in mind."

He clicked his tongue in mock disapproval. "And people call you a clever woman."

She flicked him a glance over her shoulder, as he deftly unfastened the extravagant crimson velvet dress. "Something's interfering with my mental processes."

He kissed the shoulder bared under the sagging gown and went to work on her corset. Her undergarments sported more exquisite embroidery, but he was too desperate for her to pay much attention.

Later. Next time. Tomorrow.

The future shone bright as the sun.

"Hmm, I wonder what that could be."

"No idea," she said drily, slithering out of dress, corset, petticoat and shift.

"You've been practicing," he said in admiration.

"I have no morals left." She faced him. "It's most distressing."

He paused to enjoy the lovely view, as she raised her hands to release her abundant black hair. In fine clothes, she did a fair job of acting the civilized creature. But he knew better. He always had. She was free and untamed, and her fiery spirit would light the rest of his days.

He gave another disappointed *tch*. "You must still cling to a few morals. You're wearing drawers."

Her narrow-eyed look didn't hide her burgeoning excitement. "Not for long, I'm sure. Isn't it time you removed a garment or two?"

He laughed. Partly at her audacity. Mostly because he was just so bloody happy. "Devil take you, you're a demanding wench. Don't you want me to woo you?"

Her smile was sizzling seduction. He'd thought he already tested the limits of arousal, but the wanton invitation in her expression made his cock swell massively against his trousers. "Of course."

He paused in pulling off his shirt. "Really?"

With greedy hands, she reached for the buttons on his trousers. "Later."

He gasped as she opened the front fall and curled her fingers around him. She didn't linger past a few breathtaking caresses. Soon he was naked, and her drawers lay white and sheer on the carpet.

Backing her toward the bed, he kissed her. What a fool he'd been to imagine he could live without this. He pushed her onto the mattress and came down over her. Lacing his fingers through hers, he slid her hands high and pressed them into the pillows near her head.

Helena raised her knees to frame his hips. Her eyes held no hesitation, just joy.

"Don't make me wait. I feel like I've already waited a

century." Her light tone cracked, and he realized that she, too, ached for the transcendent joining.

West tightened his hips and plunged into her. She cried out and clenched hard around him. He went still, letting the radiance seep into his bones.

He felt entirely possessed, united with Helena in a way not even their most passionate earlier encounters had achieved. Knowing that she gave herself without condition or limit transformed the physical act into a mysterious connection he'd never experienced before.

At last, he moved, and on another cry, she convulsed. He rose on his arms to watch her swift climax. She arched against the sheets, quivering with ecstasy. As she started to come down off that shuddering peak, his kiss promised her forever.

Then blindly he sought his own release. Driving into her hard to stamp his claim on her. She moaned and rose to meet every thrust.

She was his. He was hers. At the height of the union, there was no difference.

He released her hands to hold her hips. The rake of her nails down his back was like a streak of lightning through the storm.

West didn't last long. He wanted her too much, and he'd been too sure that he'd lost her. The mighty surge began in the soles of his feet, blazed up through his legs, and centered on his burning balls. He gave a guttural groan as his seed burst forth into her welcoming body.

Gasping, he slumped over her, crushing her beneath him. Then with his last strength, he rolled to the side and separated their sweat-slicked bodies.

Never before had he given so much to a woman. Masculine satisfaction flooded him as he relished the idea that they might have started a child.

The air was thick with the scent of sex. In the early February dusk, Helena's lithe form gleamed white and beautiful. Her hair snaked around her as she lay sprawled against the sheets. She looked exhausted and well used, but contented in a way he'd never seen her before.

When his pulse had calmed, he caught the hand lying loose and open on the sheets and raised it to his lips. "I'll use more finesse next time."

Her laugh was a soft puff of weariness. "I'm beginning to think finesse might be overrated."

"I'll look forward to convincing you otherwise."

Her free hand gave a floppy wave. "I'll have to marry you now."

"If you don't, I want Artemis back."

"There is that." Then contrary to her teasing, she turned to curve one arm around his neck and kiss him as if his presence was as necessary as air.

"Come here," he muttered, and drew her close. She rested her dark head on his chest and curled into his side.

For a long time, they lay in the gathering twilight. Gradually West's heart found its natural rhythm.

He spoke the words he'd kept hidden for more than a year. "I'm sure a woman of your enormous intellect has already worked out that I love you."

The silence that greeted his declaration seemed to last a month.

Then she rose on her elbow to study him through the shadows, her eyes like a starlit night. "Of course I hoped. Especially once you started acting like a hero, afire to save my honor and sacrifice yourself for my happiness."

He gave her a sheepish smile. "The result of temporary madness. I promise to return to being a selfish swine forthwith."

She smiled back and ran her hand down his jaw with a tenderness that made him ache. "The problem, West, is that for a woman of such vaunted intelligence, I've always misunderstood you. I think it's because you stole my heart when I was a silly girl, and I never got it back."

Stole her heart? He brightened. That sounded damned promising.

Attempting his old sardonic manner, he arched an eyebrow. "You weren't a silly girl. You were smart enough to choose me."

She kissed him softly. "I was, wasn't I? But not smart enough to see that under your arrogance, you were a man of honor. And I should have seen that. Even when I was sixteen and mad about you, you restricted yourself to a few kisses, although you must have known I was ripe for seduction. Crewe certainly knew."

West didn't want to talk about her vile husband. Not now when she said things that made him hope. "You were my best friend's sister."

"See what I mean? And you've verged on Sir Galahad in the last few days. Bone-headed, I think you'll agree, but unwaveringly gallant."

"Would you rather have a clever cad?"

Another of those bewitching, enigmatic smiles. "Cads don't go the distance, in my view. I'm all for knights in shining armor these days, even when they choose to wear a bedsheet instead."

With care, he picked his way through her words. This was too important for him to get wrong. "So you've decided you like me?"

A brief laugh. "I'd better, given what we just did."

"And you want me?"

"Oh, yes, that's in no doubt."

Devil take her, why wouldn't she say it? "And do you think you can bring yourself to call me Vernon?"

She frowned. "That seems very intimate."

"Damn it, Helena," he growled.

Her hand rested above his thundering heart. "Will you give me Artemis?"

"She's been yours from the start."

She lowered her eyes. "In that case, there's no hiding the sad truth."

Tension filled him. "Sad truth?"

Helena shook the mane of hair back from her face and grinned at him with all the mischief of her childhood self. A mischief the years had almost ripped away from her.

"Yes, the sad truth that I'm head over heels."

That was close, but not close enough. When he covered her hand with his, the contact radiated through him. He was counted a brave man, but it took all his courage to take the next step. "Say it, Helena."

His ruthlessness sparked a flash of excitement in her eyes. Then her expression turned serious, and at last she opened the gates of her soul to him. He read the answer in her face before she spoke. Although when they came, the words were sweeter than honey.

"I love you, Vernon. I'll love you forever."

EPILOGUE

Grosvenor Square, London, February 1825

*I*n Caroline's opulent drawing room, Helena sat in her usual place by the hearth and studied her friends. Dashing Widows no more, but vibrant, fulfilled women who had found love and happiness and purpose.

"What is it, Hel?" Fen asked, sensitive as ever. She still took charge of the tea table to save the Meissen china, although these days, various offspring posed a greater threat to the porcelain than Caro's dramatic gestures.

Helena gave her a smile. "I was thinking that it's almost five years to the day since we swore to set the ton on its ear."

"We succeeded," Fen said, smiling back.

"You certainly did, Lady Kenwick."

Not long after marrying Fenella, Anthony had received an earldom, and he was now acknowledged as a major power in government. Gentle Fenella had unexpectedly emerged as an influential political hostess. Her ability to bring warring sides together had become legendary.

"We also swore never to marry," Caro said drily from where she stood near the window. Against the blue and gold brocade curtains, her body was round with pregnancy.

She'd returned from an exciting, sometimes dangerous year in China with the news that she'd conceived. Her daughter Roberta, a rambunctious two-year-old, played upstairs in the nursery with Fenella's baby son Henry, and Helena's three-year-old twins, Margaret and Silas.

As her husband had suspected, Helena's fears of barrenness had proven unfounded. In a secretive gesture, her hand dropped to where another child grew. It was so soon, she hadn't told Vernon yet, although something in Fenella's blue eyes hinted that she guessed the secret.

"You can't say you're sorry," Helena said. "We won't believe you."

Caro and Silas split their time between Woodley Park and this house, when Silas wasn't traveling with his family to lecture, or search out new species. His cherry tree, the *Caroline Nash*, promised to cause a sensation on its commercial release next year.

Since her marriage, Caro's dreams of seeing the world had become reality. This afternoon tea was a rare reunion. Caro and Silas had recently returned from Madagascar. Anthony was in London for meetings, and he'd brought Fen and the children up to Town with him.

Caro stared out into the street with sudden interest, and she answered Helena without turning around. "I wouldn't dare. I still run in terror of your sharp tongue."

Helena made a dismissive noise. "These days, I'm so domesticated, I can barely summon a critical word." Proving herself wrong, she asked, "What on earth has you grinning like a loon into thin air?"

"Our men are back."

Noise in the hallway outside heralded a tumble of vigorous masculine bodies into the feminine space. Silas, tall and rumpled and full of life. Anthony, large and steadfast. Brandon Deerham and his best friend Carey Townsend, both at sixteen on the verge of manhood.

Last and most beloved of all, her dearest Vernon. Tall, dark, and devilishly handsome. The silver frosting his black hair added maturity to his spectacular features. Recurring bouts of fever had taken their toll, but, thank God, during the last two years they'd become more infrequent. He hadn't suffered a relapse in six months, the longest respite they'd had. Helena cautiously hoped that the worst was over.

His glinting green gaze found hers. The bond between them still thrilled her. She only had to think back to herself five years ago—to the others, also—to realize how generously the years had treated them. Anticipating his pleasure when she told him about the baby, she sent Vernon a private smile.

"Mamma," Brandon said, loping toward Fen on his long legs. Like his half-brother Henry, he was golden fair and bore the look of his mother. "Uncle Vernon is giving Carey and me our choice of colts from this year's foals. Isn't that grand?"

"We trounced them into the ground, and that was the deal," Carey stated emphatically. Along with his swarthy looks, he'd inherited his uncle's forceful character.

Fenella turned aghast to Helena's husband. "Vernon, that's too much."

He shook his head as he crossed to kiss his wife and lounge on the arm of her chair. "They had a devil of a convincing win at football. A bet is a bet."

Since marrying, Helena and Vernon had become infrequent visitors to the capital. They spent most of their time at Shelton Abbey, raising the best horses in the country. Or so Helena proudly believed. That opinion had some justification. Artemis's first foal had won last year's Derby by a length and a half.

Nor had Helena given up her charity schools or

mathematical work. Earlier this year, she'd started correspondence with an enterprising young man called Charles Babbage, who had plans to design a universal calculating machine. The possibilities were intriguing.

"I hope you both said thank you." When Fen glanced at Anthony, he shrugged his helplessness to interfere.

"They played a right bonny game," he said in his rumbling bass.

"They must have," Fen retorted.

"Where are the holy terrors?" Silas asked, looking around.

"Upstairs with their nurses," Caro said. "We couldn't get a moment's peace with them here. And it's such an age since I saw Fen and Hel."

"I'll go up and release them from captivity," Helena said, rising swiftly. Too swiftly. The room wavered in front of her, and she wobbled on her feet. "Oh, dear—"

"Helena?" Vernon leaped to his feet and whipped his arm around her waist.

She gulped for air as everyone crowded around, until Fenella, bless her, came to the rescue. "For heaven's sake, step back, and let the poor woman breathe."

"Aren't you well, darling?" Vernon asked in concern.

Helena licked dry lips and struggled to form reassuring words, but Fenella beat her to it. "Of course she's well. But now she's in a delicate condition, she needs to stop bounding around like an overexcited kangaroo."

"Delicate—"

Helena returned to herself in time to see his puzzlement vanish under a flood of delight. "Another baby?"

She nodded, overjoyed with his joy. "In late August, I think."

"My love, you make me so damned happy." Despite their audience, he caught her up in his arms and kissed her until she was dizzier than ever.

ABOUT THE AUTHOR

ANNA CAMPBELL has written 10 multi award-winning historical romances for Grand Central Publishing and Avon HarperCollins, and her work is published in 22 languages. She has also written 21 bestselling independently published romances, including her series, The Dashing Widows and The Lairds Most Likely. Anna has won numerous awards for her Regency-set stories including Romantic Times Reviewers Choice, the Booksellers Best, the Golden Quill (three times), the Heart of Excellence (twice), the Write Touch, the Aspen Gold (twice) and the Australian Romance Readers Association's favorite historical romance (five times). Her books have three times been nominated for Romance Writers of America's prestigious RITA Award, and three times for Australia's Romantic Book of the Year. When she's not traveling the world seeking inspiration for her stories, Anna lives on the beautiful east coast of Australia.

Anna loves to hear from her readers. You can find her at:

Website: www.annacampbell.com

ALSO BY ANNA CAMPBELL

Claiming the Courtesan

Untouched

Tempt the Devil

Captive of Sin

My Reckless Surrender

Midnight's Wild Passion

The Sons of Sin series:

Seven Nights in a Rogue's Bed

Days of Rakes and Roses

A Rake's Midnight Kiss

What a Duke Dares

A Scoundrel by Moonlight

Three Proposals and a Scandal

The Dashing Widows:

The Seduction of Lord Stone

Tempting Mr. Townsend

Winning Lord West

Pursuing Lord Pascal

Charming Sir Charles

Catching Captain Nash

Lord Garson's Bride

The Lairds Most Likely:

The Laird's Willful Lass

The Laird's Christmas Kiss

The Highlander's Lost Lady

Christmas Stories:

The Winter Wife

Her Christmas Earl

A Pirate for Christmas

Mistletoe and the Major

A Match Made in Mistletoe

The Christmas Stranger

Other Books:

These Haunted Hearts

Stranded with the Scottish Earl

THE SEDUCTION OF LORD STONE

(The Dashing Widows Book 1)

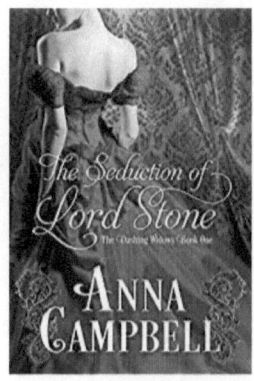

For this reckless widow, love is the most dangerous game of all.

Caroline, Lady Beaumont, arrives in London seeking excitement after ten dreary years of marriage and an even drearier year of mourning. That means conquering society, dancing like there's no tomorrow, and taking a lover to provide passion without promises. Promises, in this dashing widow's dictionary, equal prison. So what is an adventurous lady to do when she loses her heart to a notorious rake who, for the first time in his life, wants forever?

Devilish Silas Nash, Viscount Stone is in love at last with a beautiful, headstrong widow bent on playing the field. Worse, she's enlisted his help to set her up with his disreputable best friend. No red-blooded man takes such a challenge lying down, and Silas schemes to seduce his darling into his arms, warm, willing and besotted. But will his passionate plots come undone against a woman determined to act the mistress, but never the wife?

TEMPTING MR TOWNSEND

(The Dashing Widows Book 2)

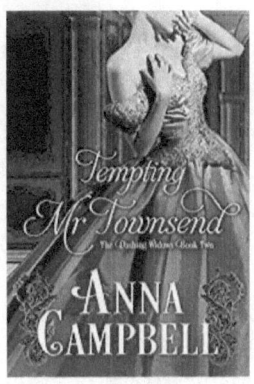

Beauty...

Fenella, Lady Deerham has rejoined society after five years of mourning her beloved husband's death at Waterloo. Now she's fêted as a diamond of the first water and London's perfect lady. But beneath her exquisite exterior, this delicate blond beauty conceals depths of courage and passion nobody has ever suspected. When her son and his school friend go missing, she vows to find them whatever it takes. Including setting off alone in the middle of the night with high-handed bear of a man, Anthony Townsend.

Will this tumultuous journey end in more tragedy? Or will the impetuous quest astonish this Dashing Widow with a breathtaking new love, and life with the last man she ever imagined?

And the Beast?

When Anthony Townsend bursts into Lady Deerham's fashionable Mayfair mansion demanding the return of his orphaned nephew, the lovely widow's beauty and spirit turn his world upside down. But surely such a refined and aristocratic creature will scorn a rough, self-made man's courtship, even if that man is now one of the richest magnates in England. Especially after he's made such a woeful first impression by barging into her house and accusing her of conniving with the runaways. But when Fenella insists on sharing the desperate search for the boys, fate offers Anthony a chance to play the hero and change her mind about him.

Will reluctant proximity convince Fenella that perhaps Mr. Townsend isn't so beastly after all? Or now that their charges are safe, will Anthony and Fenella remain forever opposites fighting their attraction?

PURSUING LORD PASCAL

(The Dashing Widows Book 4)

Golden Days...

Famous for her agricultural innovations, Amy, Lady Mowbray has never had a romantical thought in her life. Well, apart from her short-lived crush on London's handsomest man, Lord Pascal, when she was a brainless 14-year-old. She even chose her late husband because he owned the best herd of beef cattle in England!

But fate steps in and waltzes this practical widow out of her rustic retreat into the glamour of the London season. When Pascal pursues her, all her adolescent fantasies come true. Those fantasies turn disturbingly adult when grown-up desire enters the equation. Amy plunges headlong into a reckless affair that promises pleasure beyond her wildest dreams – until she discovers that this glittering world hides damaging secrets and painful revelations set to break a country girl's tender heart.

All that glitters...

Gervaise Dacre, Lord Pascal needs to marry money to save his estate, devastated after a violent storm. He's never much liked his reputation as London's handsomest man, but it certainly comes in handy when the time arrives to seek a rich bride. Unfortunately, the current crop of debutantes bores him silly, and he finds himself praying for a sensible woman with a generous dowry.

When he meets Dashing Widow Amy Mowbray, it seems all his prayers have been answered. Until he finds himself in thrall to the lovely widow, and his mercenary quest becomes dangerously complicated. Soon he's much more interested in passion than in pounds, shillings and pence. What happens if Amy discovers the sordid truth behind his whirlwind courtship? And if she does, will she see beyond his original, selfish motives to the ardent love that lies unspoken in his sinful heart?

CHARMING SIR CHARLES

(The Dashing Widows Book 5)

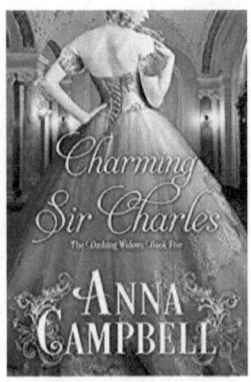

Matchmaking mayhem in Mayfair!

Sally Cowan, Countess of Norwood, spent ten miserable years married to an overbearing oaf. Now she's free, she plans to have some fun. But before she kicks her heels up, this Dashing Widow sets out to launch her pretty, headstrong niece Meg into society and find her a good husband.

When rich and charming Sir Charles Kinglake gives every sign that he can't get enough of Meg's company, Sally is delighted to play chaperone at all their meetings. Charles is everything that's desirable in a gentleman suitor. How disastrous, when over the course of the season's most elegant house party, Sally realizes that desire is precisely the name of the game. She's found her niece's perfect match—but she wants him for herself!

There are none so blind as those who will not see...

From the moment Sir Charles Kinglake meets sparkling Lady Norwood, he's smitten. He courts her as a gentleman should—dancing with her at every glittering ball, taking her to the theatre, escorting her around London. Because she's acting as chaperone to her niece, that means most times, Meg accompanies them. The lack of privacy chafes a man consumed by desire, but Charles's intentions are honorable, and he's willing to work within the rules to win the wife he wants.

However when he discovers that his careful pursuit has convinced Sally he's interested in Meg rather than her, he flings the rules out the window. When love is at stake, who cares about a little scandal? It's time for charming Sir Charles to abandon the subtle approach and play the passionate lover, not the society suitor!

Now with everything at sixes and sevens, Sir Charles risks everything to show lovely Lady Norwood they make the perfect pair!

CATCHING CAPTAIN NASH

(The Dashing Widows Book 6)

Home is the sailor, home from the sea...

Five years after he's lost off the coast of South America, presumed dead, Captain Robert Nash escapes cruel captivity, and returns to London and the bride he loves, but barely knows. When he stumbles back into the family home, he's appalled to find himself gate-crashing the party celebrating his wife's engagement to another man.

This gallant naval officer is ready to take on any challenge; but five years is a long time, and beautiful, passionate Morwenna has clearly found a life without him. Can he win back the wife who gave him a reason to survive his ordeal? Or will the woman who haunts his every thought remain eternally out of reach?

Love lost and found? Or love lost forever?

Since hearing of her beloved husband's death, Morwenna

Nash has been mired in grief. After five bleak years without him, she must summon every ounce of courage and determination to become a Dashing Widow and rejoin the social whirl. She owes it to her young daughter to break free of old sorrow and find a new purpose in life, even if that means accepting a loveless marriage.

It's a miracle when Robert returns from the grave, and despite the awkward circumstances of his arrival, she's overjoyed that her husband has come back to her at last. But after years of suffering, he's not the handsome, laughing charmer she remembers. Instead he's a grim shadow of his former dashing self. He can't hide how much he still wants her—but does passion equal love?

Can Morwenna and Robert bridge the chasm of absence, suffering and mistrust, and find their way back to each other?

LORD GARSON'S BRIDE

(The Dashing Widows Book 7)

Lord Garson's dilemma.

Hugh Rutherford, Lord Garson, loved and lost when his fiancée returned to the husband she'd believed drowned. In the three years since, Garson has come to loathe his notoriety as London's most famous rejected suitor. It's high time to find a bride, a level-headed, well-bred lady who will accept a loveless marriage and cause no trouble. Luckily he has just the candidate in mind.

A marriage of convenience...

When Lady Jane Norris receives an unexpected proposal from her childhood friend Lord Garson, marriage to the handsome baron rescues her from a grim future. At twenty-eight, Jane is on the shelf and under no illusions about her attractions. With her father's death, she's lost her home and faces life as an impecunious spinster. While she's aware

Garson will never love again, they have friendship and goodwill to build upon. What can possibly go wrong?

...becomes very inconvenient indeed.

From the first, things don't go to plan, not least because Garson soon finds himself in thrall to his surprisingly intriguing bride. A union grounded in duty veers toward obsession. And when the Dashing Widows take Jane in hand and transform her into the toast of London, Garson isn't the only man to notice his wife's beauty and charm. He's known Jane all her life, but suddenly she's a dazzling stranger. This isn't the uncomplicated, pragmatic match he signed up for. When Jane defies the final taboo and asks for his love, her impossible demand threatens to blast this convenient marriage to oblivion.

Once the dust settles, will Lord Garson still be the man who can only love once?